BOUND TO SECRECY

'The irritation and frustrations of the main character create vortices of Shakespearean intensity' **Berliner Zeitung**

'He succeeds in letting an African detective fail in an African way. And both the story and the failure are grandiose' **Deutsche Welle**

'I choose to call Bound to Secrecy a 'great literature', because Vamba Sherif writes in a concise, impressive style; he eschews philosophical and psychological treats, and like all good novelists, he lets his story, his "heroes" live through their actions' **Readme**

'Sherif's novel is written in a concise, accurate and relentless language…. The writer plays confidently with the classics of world literature' **Mannheimer Morgen**

Vamba Sherif was born in Kolahun, Liberia in 1973. In his early teens he moved to Kuwait, where he completed secondary school. The First Gulf War compelled him to leave Kuwait and settle first in Damascus, Syria, and then in The Netherlands, where he read Law. Vamba is also a journalist and film critic. His passions include music, film and rare books on Africa. His books include: *The Land of The Fathers, The Kingdom of Sebah, The Witness* and *The Black Napoleon*.

BOUND TO SECRECY

Vamba Sherif

hoperoad : London

HopeRoad Publishing Ltd
P O Box 55544
Exhibition Road
London SW7 2DB

www.hoperoadpublishing.com
First published by HopeRoad 2015

The right of Vamba Sherif to be identified as author of this work has been asserted in accordance with Section 77 of the Copyright, Designs and Patents Act 1988

Copyright © 2006 Vamba Sherif

A CIP catalogue for this book is available from the British Library

All rights reserved. No part of this book may be reproduced, stored in a retrieval system or transmitted in any form or by any means, electronic, mechanical, photocopying, recording or otherwise, without the prior permission of the publisher.

ISBN 978-1-908446-32-9

eISBN 978-1-908446-38-1

Printed and bound by
Lightning Source

To the women of Liberia who inspired this book

CHAPTER 1

On an oppressive day in the dry season, a man stepped off a bus and crossed the main street of the border town of Wologizi. He approached a young man who was bending over a cistern filled with water. The youth had been gazing for quite some time at his own reflection, and the face that greeted him in the clear water wore a beatific smile. Though the stranger walked with a limp, over the years he had learned to conceal his handicap cleverly by strutting, so that the youth who heard his footsteps and turned fully to face him assumed he was arrogant. In fact, the youth was less fascinated by his suitcase or tailored, three-piece suit than by his manner of walking. It was the assertive gait of a man well aware of the effect his appearance had on people.

The stranger sat down on a bench under a leafy tree not far from the youth, and he heaved a deep sigh that betrayed his contentment. Wologizi fulfilled his expectations, for as he glanced across the dusty street, he could see several old men: two of them were stretched out in hammocks, and the others were lying on mats, whiling away the stifling hours in the shade of a breadfruit tree. The border town was asleep, in the thrall of the heat. While travelling to the town, the stranger had toyed with the idea of yielding, like those old men did, to the lethargic spell of the heat without a care in the world. And as if to confirm that thought, a gentle breeze started from his right, from the direction of the youth, and drifted peacefully towards him. He closed his eyes to savour it to the full.

'Come here,' he called to the young man.

The stranger watched him cover the short distance between them, his gestures languid, his gait remarkably feline, but not until the youth stood before him did he notice the fear in his eyes.

'Can you show me the way to the mansion?'

This was how the house was called in that part of the country, the mansion, and the stranger knew this. The youth raised a slender hand and pointed to a house in the far distance. The hand, the stranger noticed, was pocked with burn marks, which did not appear to be ritualistic, but he stood up, choosing to ignore them. Beyond an ochre hill through which the main road had been carved, the stranger could see the mansion perched proudly on another hilltop.

'Who lives there?' he asked.

The youth did not answer.

'Tell me who lives there?' he insisted.

Although the identity of the occupant of the mansion was common knowledge, the youth remained silent.

'Come on, don't be afraid. Tell me.'

The stranger's tone was reassuring, even appealing, but the young man continued staring at the ground. Perhaps, the stranger thought, the young man's reluctance was due to his timidity.

'Why are you so silent?'

It was at this point that he reached out to pat the young man on the shoulder, a gesture he immediately regretted, for it triggered a reaction that baffled him. The youth recoiled, broke into a run, and never looked back until he disappeared behind a curtain of dust.

The incident still disturbed the stranger even after he had traded the pleasant shade for the terrible heat, and when he turned to the old men he saw that they had not stirred from their positions.

The road he took to the mansion was punctuated by dust-swathed houses, from which an occasional voice could be heard, subdued to an almost sensual whisper by the noonday heat. On reaching the town centre proper, he saw a Lebanese man, one of many who traded in that country, standing before his shop and munching a loaf of bread with the avarice of a child. On his right, he saw several youngsters gathered around a poster, in front of a cinema, discussing the film – its heroes and heroines and the murderous tactics of its villains. It reminded him of his own childhood. The stranger passed a gas station where some men were playing checkers beneath its rusty roof. Incited by a handful of spectators, the two main players were slandering and insulting each other, cursing and swearing in the most exaggerated tones, as if locked in a duel of death. The first threatened to defeat the second, warning that he would forfeit his wife and property to the winner and never play checkers again. The stranger ignored them, but could still feel their eyes boring a hole in his back, even after he'd rounded a bend. On turning around, certain he would face one of them, he saw nothing but a cloud of dust rapidly heading his way.

Soon, he arrived at a junction with divergent paths which went on to enclose collections of thatched huts and mud and brick houses. Instead of taking the road to the mansion, he opted for the main one that led up a mountain and down a valley. He wanted to see the river that formed the border between his country and the other, and how the border was manned. However, the ascent was difficult, the heat unbearable, and soon he was sweating profusely. The stranger loathed the smell of his own sweat, which was acrid now despite the fragrance that he wore, and more than once he had to stop to dab his face with a handkerchief.

It took him nearly an hour to reach the river which lay at the foot of the mountain. Long before he could see it he could hear it gurgling softly, as though it was whispering a secret. Contrary to his expectation, there was no building on either side of the river to indicate where one boundary ended and the other began, no custom officers, in fact no sign of life at all but an occasional call of a lone bird or an animal. Even the river was carelessly bridged. Some logs had been thrown across it, which were now old and worn out. Beside the bridge, tied to the trunk of one giant tree and extended across the river to another, were strings of woven ropes, a phenomenon known in that part of the country as the monkey-bridge, a bridge used only during rainy season when the river overflowed and covered the main bridge. What manner of a border town was it without clear-cut borders?

The stranger turned back and headed for the mansion. Long before he could reach it, the house rose before him, majestic and imposing, overlooking Wologizi with evident pomposity. The three-story building was cut off from all sides – from the valley at its rear and the town sprawled below it – by walls of cement bricks topped with shards of bottles. The first thing that caught his attention was the radio antenna which towered over the house. Then he saw a warning boldly written on the gate which read: **BEWARE OF MY PRESENCE**. He reasoned that perhaps it referred to a ferocious canine trained to pounce on intruders like him, so he shouted to lure it out but got no response.

On drawing closer to the legend, he noticed that unlike the rest of the walls it had been repainted recently. The gate stood open, and he entered with some reluctance. On his right was the one room-radio station which he approached, listening for any sign of movement. It had no door and its windows were broken. The stranger entered and discovered that the radio which connected Wologizi with the outside world was out of order. All of a sudden he had a distinct feeling that someone was spying on him, and he left the radio station as if in a daze.

Climbing the stairs up to the first floor of the house, he emerged into a spacious living room with a high ceiling, stained at the corners as a result of leakages. Everything was covered with dust: the once beautiful chairs and tables with the flag and seal of the country carved with precision in them, the wooden cupboards with an impressive display of Chinese porcelains and vases, and the gilt-framed portraits of various dignitaries, were all entangled in mass of cobwebs. Even the walls were not spared. Spiders were perched in many corners, the windowpanes grimmy. The smell of decay lingered in the air, dominant and pervasive, and for a while the stranger stood still, taking in that neglected splendour, overwhelmed by it all.

Outside, at the rear of the house, he searched for an explanation for the condition of the mansion but was offered none. There was a kitchen without utensils, and a well beside which stood a rusty bucket. He paused to gaze at a mountain rising up before him, just one of a long chain of colossal mountains that enclosed Wologizi.

Once again he felt a presence behind him, furtive but persistent, and he turned around only to face a tiny, emaciated old man in a homespun baggy gown, his jaws moving determinedly as he chewed a kolanut. The old man looked wary of the stranger. The sun was at its zenith now, beating down with cruel intensity on the two men; the air was still, trapped momentarily in the oppressive silence of that deserted place.

'What a beautiful mansion you've got here,' the stranger said.

To this unusual form of introduction, the old man initially responded with silence but could not resist the disarming smile of the stranger who moved towards him, his hand stretched out in a greeting.

'That's what everyone who comes to Wologizi says.'

The stranger's handshake was firm, and as it tightened around his hand, the old man felt an unbearable pain but chose to conceal it.

'One cannot miss it,' the man went on, his voice carrying the same note of spontaneity and charm as at first. 'When I stepped off the bus I saw it in the distance and decided to admire it from close.'

Only then did he let go of the old man's hand, and he quickly moved to the front of the compound where he stood gazing with rapture at the mansion, as if he was seeing it for the first time.

'It looks so out of place here,' he finally said.

'The mansion was built a long time ago for the president who's yet to visit us and occupy it. Until then we've decided to keep it empty. Every once in a while we come up here to dust it.'

The old man, as he said this, noted the stranger's every reaction but apart from the warm smile on his face he betrayed no other emotion.

'It's indeed a house befitting a president.'

The old man moved a few paces away from the stranger, as if he was about to leave him, but suddenly turned to him.

'You said you stepped off the bus here?'

'I was just passing through.'

'Never been to this part of the country?'

'It's my very first time here, old man.'

'Then you should have known that a bus comes this way once every few days and sometimes once a week.'

'Once every few days?' the stranger asked.

The old man nodded. The two were standing under an acacia tree, facing the radio antenna to which the stranger's eyes often turned, as if wondering about its relevance to Wologizi. In silence both men pondered the exchange, each lost in his world, each weighing what to say next, and then one of them spoke: 'There is nothing I crave right now in this unbearable heat more than a cold palm wine.'

It was the stranger. This frankness brought a smile to the old man's face, for it confirmed what he'd been thinking at that every moment.

'Then you've come to the right place,' he said.

Both men laughed. The sun was at their backs, fierce and implacable, as they climbed down the hill.

On the roadside, in front of them, a snake lay basking in the sunlight, but on noticing the two men it slithered into the grass, becoming one with the bush. When silence fell in the wake of the footsteps of the two men, the snake emerged out of hiding and glided languidly to the roadside.

Wologizi was still in the grasp of the heat, but in a few hours it would shed off this numbing influence and usher in the evening with a flurry of activities.

CHAPTER 2

To do justice to the palm wine, the two men began with four gourds which stood on a beautifully carved stool between them. They were seated in collapsible chairs under a mango tree and drank from a small calabash. First, the stranger took a large swig, and the old man who watched him thought he would empty the calabash in one gulp, but then he stopped. 'Palm wine is the nectar of the gods,' he said as though it was a revelation, and then passed the calabash to the old man, wiping his mouth with a handkerchief. The old man agreed. 'There's nothing like it,' he said, and drained the rest.

The men teased each other about their passion for palm wine, but with the fourth and last gourd the drinking took on a solemn aspect. The two began to appraise each other anew, each bent on making the other drunk. The stranger refilled the calabash but instead of drinking he leaned towards the old man as though to bow to him, to honour him as befitted a man of his age. The old man, who could not decline the honour, emptied the calabash in one swallow, refilled it and handed it over to the stranger. The wine was strong – the old man knew this – for it had been tapped from one of the best palm trees in Wologizi. The stranger emptied the calabash; his eyes, the old man noticed, had already glazed over, and his tongue swept across the corners of his lips, lapping up the froth, and then he broke into a laughter filled with the mystery of drunkenness. He keeled over, his whole body rocking to it.

It was time, the old man thought, to pose his question, and he did so casually. 'You said you were sent to Wologizi?'

The stranger sat up, poured some wine into the calabash, his hands trembling, visibly drunk now, but he gulped it all down.

'No,' he slurred. 'I'm just passing through.'

Then he passed the calabash to the old man who took a sip and handed it back to him, amazed by his unusual resistance to the wine.

'What was your name again?' he asked.

'William Soko Mawolo.'

The stranger answered curtly, his voice crisp, as if he had not had a single drop of wine. The name baffled the old man. Though it sounded familiar there was also something obscure about it, especially the middle name which was unfamiliar to him. The stranger was of imposing height, his skin so dark that his forehead glinted blue. He was much unlike the people of that forest region, whose skin colour was less sooty than his own. The old man concluded that he was indeed a foreigner, perhaps from beyond the borders, but on the other hand he spoke like them, drank palm wine with the same passion.

'Mine is Kapu,' the old man said. 'However, everyone in Wologizi calls me Old Kapu, and I recommend you do the same, Mr Mawolo.'

'I certainly will,' William replied, and turned his attention to the wine as if he was noticing it for the first time.

'What do you do all day, Old Kapu?'

'I don't want to bore you with the story of my work, Mr Mawolo. Suffice to say that it is very unrewarding.'

'Then why do you do it?'

Old Kapu did not answer but instead leaned back on the collapsible chair and then in a slow, calculated voice said:

'You look like a government minister to me, Mr Mawolo.'

'Far from it. I work for myself, Old Kapu.'

After taking another sip of the wine, the old man filled up the calabash and told William to drink the rest.

'Our palm wine is the very best in this region.'

The fourth gourd was empty, but William insisted that Old Kapu send someone to buy more wine.

'Don't worry, Old Kapu, I'll pay.'

The old man ordered another gourd of wine. Meanwhile, as the two waited to begin another round, the household awoke with the return of most of its members from farms or from performing daily chores. Some women were preparing food at the back of the house, and William could hear a few of them trading insults with an ease bordering on revelry. In the midst of the bustle he would turn his gaze to anyone who entered or left the house, especially the women. Whenever one greeted him William would answer in a voice so imbued with charm that the woman in question would end up bursting into laughter. 'Old Kapu's life must have changed for the better the day he laid eyes on you,' he would say if she turned out to be one of the old man's many wives. If not, he would say: 'Perhaps I'll wed you before I leave, Beauty.'

Old Kapu, amused by it all, was silent.

The women were not offended by William's conduct but would disappear in the house, giggling like young girls.

At a certain point, one of them came out to ask Old Kapu for some money to purchase food in the market the next day. She was of indeterminate age, with austerly plaited hair and cracked lips, her ample hips disproportionate to her thin body. Except for her hips, which were round like a calabash, the woman was not endowed with any particular beauty, William could see that. The wrappers that covered her tender figure were worn out, her blouse faded, but she stood before the two men aware of the stranger's gaze, basking fully in his attention. 'Fend for yourself,' her husband shouted at her in a dismissive tone.

She seemed taken aback by the sudden outburst, and was about to leave when William reached in his pocket and placed some money firmly in her hand. 'For tomorrow's food,' he said jokingly. 'But don't tell Old Kapu. Otherwise he might throw me out of his house.'

She left them, her laughter ringing like a noon bell.

'You are spoiling them, Mr Mawolo. What would I do if you were to leave tomorrow and I was left alone to face them?'

'What you do every day, Old Kapu. I'm sure that after I've left they would have forgotten I was ever here.'

The palm wine arrived as the two were dining – a sumptuous dinner that consisted of newly harvested rice and smoked meat stewed to the marrow in a sauce of wild mushrooms. The men washed down every mouthful with palm wine, but even at this point the wine did not loosen their tongues. Instead a solemn silence, forced upon them by the attention they paid to the food, lingered on long after they were finished.

Later, Old Kapu placed a pinch of snuff on his tongue and leaned backward on his chair, fully relishing the tobacco.

He must be in his seventies, William thought, still strong and wiry, unyielding to the influence of the palm wine. Most of the old man's teeth had fallen out, but he still looked young, however, and his skin was smooth, with little or no hair at all. Perhaps, William thought, such men never aged and died armed with the full vigour of a youth of twenty.

Night met William stifling a yawn, tired after a long and eventful day. The light that accompanied the night went off minutes after it had come on, throwing Wologizi into a nervous darkness. One of Old Kapu's many wives brought out a hurricane lamp and placed it on the stool between the two men, but its light was not enough to shun off the deep darkness that enveloped them. At length Old Kapu sat up and spat a generous residue of snuff in the dust.

'I'll show you to your room,' he said.

On standing up, the old man felt a shearing backache which forced him back into his chair. He let out a groan.

'The pain is like our generator,' he said at length. 'It comes and goes unexpectedly, sometimes leaving me paralysed.'

Old Kapu refused William's offer of help and waited until the pain subsided. With the hurricane lamp in his hand, he led his guest to a room which faced a long corridor that ended at the back of the compound. To the right of the door stood a grandfather clock.

'It's been out of order for years,' Old Kapu said.

'Maybe I can help you with it,' William said.

'Do you repair things?'

'It's what I do for a living.'

The room was furnished with a nylon-covered table, on which stood a hurricane lamp that cast a forlorn light around the room, giving it an eerie aspect. Most of the green painting on its walls had peeled off, and it had no window or ceiling. As a result, William could hear the women gossiping in the other rooms.

Later, one of them, the woman he'd given some money to that afternoon, knocked at his door. 'Your bath is ready,' she said.

'What is your name? I forgot to ask you this afternoon,' he said playfully.

'Hawah Lombeh,' she answered.

She was a head shorter than he was, and he noticed that she could not muster the courage to stare him in the eyes. William reached out to touch her face. It felt very coarse, inflicted by hard work and the scorching sun of that region. She pulled away in panic.

'Tell me what Old Kapu does,' he said.

She shook her head. Suddenly, so that she had no time to react, he drew her to him, and caressed her weather-beaten face until she moaned, until she could no longer refuse him or his request.

'He's the town chief,' she whispered.

That was all. Hawah Lombeh broke away from him then as though in anger, terribly distressed, and her figure receded into the darkness of the long corridor. Even when he could no longer see her could still hear her footsteps, hear her crash into something, whimpering as she regained her balance.

The bathroom was located at the far rear of the house, a shed of bamboo trees without a door, but the darkness served as cover as he squatted on a bed of pebbles. The water was pleasantly warm, and he relished every drop. Joyful shouts suddenly rose from the compound to greet the lights that had come on. Conversations that had been subdued before now became boisterous, and between the cries of children bent on attracting attention, the women related the events of the day. William listened to their voices, captivated by their warmth. They sounded so familier, plucked out of a distant past, that a sense of longing took hold of him; the longing for moments he wished he'd been raised in Wologizi and could live there forever like one of them.

It was on a night such as this, in a town such as Wologizi, that as a child he would lie awake in bed, listening to his aunt singing a song in the other room. She would throw remarks at him, which were all about seriousness, most often about how hard he had to work to excel at everything, especially at school. That was long before their smooth and predictable life came to an abrupt end.

Once inside his room, he put off the light and retired to bed, sober as if he had not had a single drop of palm wine. He listened to the voices of the gossiping women, cheerful at one moment but punctuated with melancholic tones at another, voices that were at once sensual and harsh. But, after listening to them for more than an hour, he hoped they would die down, for the radio station awaited him. William wanted to slip out of the house that night and to the mansion with the intention of repairing the radio. But every time he attempted to leave, a cough or a noise would prevent him from opening the door and crossing the long corridor out of the house. Eventually he gave up and succumbed to sleep. However, within minutes, he was jolted out of his rest by a voice, which rose in a singular, heartrending dirge, tearing the silence of the night asunder. The song continued until the small hours and stopped only when a cock finally crowed, announcing the crack of William's first dawn in Wologizi.

He'd not slept a wink.

CHAPTER 3

William waited until the entire household had awoken and someone had knocked at his door announcing his morning bath before leaving his room. The wailing voice still haunted him, and he thought that whoever had died must have been very dear to the person whose voice had filled the night with such grief. At the entrance to the bathroom he found two bucketfuls of warm water instead of the customary one ready for him, but could make neither head nor tail of the generosity. While carrying the buckets into the bathroom, he felt eyes on him, but when he turned towards the doors and windows of the houses at the rear of the compound, he saw no one. Then a female voice broke into laughter, and he understood: it was Hawah Lombeh, the woman who had betrayed her husband by revealing his occupation to William. He shouted out his gratitude to her but she pretended with her silence not to have heard him. Finished with his bath, he went to his room. It took him a while to get dressed, and later he emerged in another suit, red against a background of ochre dust and bluish sky, his sooty skin glowing in the soft, morning light.

Some children, impressed by his good looks and peculiar steps, crowded about him. They imitated that gait that marked him out everywhere, but their steps were not as supple as his, so they implored him to teach them. But he only laughed, amused at their eagerness. 'Come and lend me a hand,' he asked them instead when ready to repair the grandfather clock. Together they carried the clock out of the house and placed it on a table under the same mango tree where he'd drunk palm wine and dined with Old Kapu the other day.

The children watched him work, affected by the solemnity he brought to his work, but suddenly he stopped.

'We are going to play a game,' he said.

They all shouted their consent. The game consisted of a number of questions, he told them calmly, and anyone who answered them correctly would be treated to a bowl of hot rice pap.

'What is the name of the paramount chief?'

The children were silent, turned to each other as though they'd not understood him, and then one of them spoke:

'We cannot say, Mr Mawolo.'

'Come on, tell me.'

'They told us not to talk about him.'

Just then, the children saw Old Kapu emerge from the house to join them, and fearing his outburst they dispersed.

'So you are a man of your word.'

Old Kapu took a seat beside him, folded his baggy gown between his legs, and bit into a kolanut. The ease with which William worked impressed him. In less than an hour the old man saw the grandfather clock, which had stood still in his house for years, begin to tick the time away, as though nothing was wrong with it.

'I have a favour to ask of you,' Old Kapu said.

William, curious, nodded.

'Follow me,' the old man said.

'Tell me what it is,' William said.

There was a note of reluctance in his voice, and despite his effort to conceal it he thought that the old man noticed it, so he decided to come up with an excuse to hide this reluctance.

'I've not yet had my breakfast.'

Old Kapu bellowed at his wives who were at the rear of the compound, and in an instant one of them appeared. She was taller than the old man, but he drew himself to his full height and slapped her hard across the face, sending her crashing into the dust.

'Mr Mawolo tells me he's not had his breakfast!'

'It's not their fault,' William intervened.

Old Kapu turned to him, trembling with rage.

'I told them I would buy some rice porridge.'

This was not true. William rushed to the woman and helped her stand up. She seemed unsure whether he meant well; her face expressed both gratitude and suspicion, as if she was certain that after it was all over, he would deliver her to her husband to be thrashed again. When William apologised to her for causing her so much trouble, her suspicion was confirmed: the stranger was either from another world or was in league with her husband. Men were not to be trusted.

Old Kapu's anger was not assuaged, for he insisted that he was the host and would make sure William was fed whatever he desired. The sugared porridge materialised within the hour, and the old man joined William, bewailing the inefficiency of his women.

'They are good for nothing, Mr Mawolo.'

They swallowed the porridge while the morning sun steadily burned their backs. Once again, the old man repeated his request.

'You have to see it to understand,' he said.

Old Kapu sounded desperate, and so in the end William agreed. The two men had not gone far when they encountered a group of militiamen on the main road. The men, numbering in their dozens, carried rusty guns and wore ill-fitting khaki uniforms, heavily creased. They were drilling, raising prickly dust, their gazes vacant. Their commander, a tall, skinny man with copper-coloured face, wore a police uniform. When he saw the two men, he stopped and his brazen gaze rested on William for a while. Then he changed direction, as though he could not tolerate what he saw, bellowing commands in a raspy voice.

Wologizi was now clearly behind them, and the two were walking up an ochre-red path, steadily climbing up a hill. It was evident to William that they were heading for the mansion. From that point, Wologizi looked rustic and poor, a sharp contrast to their destination. Before the two could climb the hill to the mansion, Old Kapu veered off the path and led him towards the town hall. They crossed a field of high, dewy grass and entered a building which smelled of gasoline.

'This is the generator which supplies Wologizi with electricity,' Old Kapu said. 'It's been repaired many times in the past but the same problem keeps recurring: it keeps switching itself on and off.'

Old Kapu threw William a glance, but because the latter chose to remain silent, he added: 'I want you to repair it, Mr Mawolo.'

William shook his head. 'I don't think I can,' he said.

'I've seen what you can do.'

William circled the machine, deep in thought, and when he circled it again he paused and heaved a long sigh, as though he'd arrived at a difficult but inevitable decision.

'If I'm to repair the generator,' he said, staring Old Kapu square in the face, 'I would need to be here day and night.'

Old Kapu seemed beside himself with joy.

'That can be easily arranged, Mr Mawolo. You can stay at the mansion for the period it takes to repair the generator. I'll go to town to ask some women to prepare the house for you. It'll be ready before sunset,' the old man said, and as a gesture of appreciation he patted William on the shoulder before leaving.

William went up to the mansion and waited under the acacia tree for the women, but they failed to appear within the hour, and so he took off his coat and set to work. First he swept the front of the house, and then hauled water from the nearby well in which he soaked some rags and went on to clean the living room. He was so immersed in his work that he did not notice the young woman until she coughed to attract his attention. When he turned, he saw her standing in the path of sunlight which streamed in a single shaft through the main door, lighting up her amber-coloured skin. She lifted her gaze and locked it firmly with the pair of male eyes that feasted on her, that glided along the contours of her slender body. He heaved a sigh akin to a moan, and when he caught a whiff of her scent it fired his imagination, for it was at once as delicious as the smell of fresh, hand-crushed flowers.

'We've come to tidy up the mansion,' she said.

She went to work immediately, assisted by a bevy of young women. The cleaning lasted for more than three hours. William, anxious to settle in that huge mansion, to make it his home, and from there go about his work, hurried the women on. 'With this pace it'll take you days to finish,' he said. The remark was intended to elicit a response from the young woman, but it failed because she was doing her best to avoid him. There was something elusive about her, he thought, a distance he could not bridge. Moreover she apparently managed to slip out of the house before all the others.

William was standing at the window on the second floor and watching each of them leave, but there was no sign of her. Silence settled on the mansion after their departure, and he went upstairs to admire the result of their work. The rooms exuded the scent of a habitable place, the spiders were gone. Each room was furnished with the same kind of exquisite chairs and tables as in the living room downstairs, and each was adorned with a large portrait of the president. In one of the rooms, the largest in the entire mansion, was a life-size portrait of the president. It dominated the room like an ever-expanding presence.

It was in this room that he encountered her. She was sitting on a king-sized bed, her hands folded on her lap, her head held up, borne by a cylinder-shaped neck with beauty lines, and she was gazing at him.

'I know why you are here,' she said.

There was a crisp edge to her voice that captivated him as much as her beauty, and he marvelled at her calmness.

'What are you talking about?'

'The moment I heard the town-crier calling on all the young women to help with cleaning the mansion, I knew that its occupant must be the person the town has been expecting.'

She laughed then, and to William her laughter sounded like a mockery, when in fact it was to compliment herself on correctly guessing the purpose of his being in that border town.

'I'm listening,' he said.

'You came to investigate the disappearance of the paramount chief,' she said, and he caught a crack in her voice.

'What if that was the case?'

'Then I warn you to be very careful.'

'Why should I be?'

She was silent; her hands were not resting on her lap any more but she'd leaned backwards against the bed, her arms supporting her, her breasts straining against her tight colourful clothes.

'Tell me about the paramount chief.'

She sat up and shrugged.

'Paramount chief Tetese is like any leader, hated and loved by his people. That's his story. It's nothing uncommon.'

'How did he disappear?'

She broke into laughter as though she was about to tell him the oddest thing he'd ever heard, and that proved to be the case.

'Rumour has it that our paramount chief Tetese was being carried in a hammock when he vanished into thin air.'

William pondered on this revelation. A hammock was an ancient form of transportation, so why did Tetese choose it and nothing else as his sole means of transportation? Moreover, the vanishing act troubled him, for a man did not just vanish in such a way.

'Who were his carriers?'

'I don't know,' she answered.

She sounded exasperated, almost angry with him, as if those were questions others had to answer, not her.

'Yet you say he was being borne in a hammock.'

'That's what I heard.'

'Why are you telling me all this?'

'Because he was my father.'

'I see,' William said, 'I see.'

It was all he could do not to conceal his utter amazement at this revelation. Her name, she told him, was Makemeh.

She left the room then, and he followed her out into the fierce sun. On her way to the gate, about to leave him, she told him that from that day onward she would be solely responsible for his culinary demands.

'What do you mean?'

She turned and took a few steps towards him.

'Do you know the most effective way people employ to get rid of their enemies in this forest region, Mr Mawolo?'

He shook his head, confused.

'They poison their food.'

She sounded matter of fact, almost uncompromising, and he watched her disappear behind the heavy gate, leaving him shivering in the chilling aftermath of her words. Seated under the acacia tree, he realised how wary he was of her but also how much he longed to see her. Just minutes after she was gone it became apparent to him that he was incapable of waiting to see her again and he rushed down the hill after her in hot pursuit.

CHAPTER 4

Makemeh was the only one besides him walking on the main street. At that hour of the day, the street exuded the sensual smell of dust as after a slight rainfall. She reached the town centre proper which was crowded with marketeers, and all the while William followed her but at a discreet distance. Soon the centre was behind them, and he saw a man approaching Makemeh with swift steps, saw him reach out to stop her by placing his hand on her shoulder. The man was tall and heavy-set like a wrestler, and he wore a tailored grey suit and a broad-brimmed white hat. From where he stood, William could not tell whether Makemeh was responding in any way to the man, as she was standing with her back to him. Suddenly she left him and walked on.

William waited, just like the man, until she veered off the main road and took a grassy path, climbing a hill towards a house he would later come to know was her home. Then the man crossed the road and entered a carpenter shop from where the sounds of machines emerged. On both sides of the path Makemeh had chosen were verdant bushes, and at one point she stepped into the bush to the right of the path. William pursued her at a quick pace but lost track of her when she stepped into the bush. He found himself in a coffee farm which encompassed a huge area, including some parts of the mountains. Fiery ants assaulted him. One got lost somewhere between his waist and nape, and just as he was about to give up after a thorough search the ant bit him. He fumbled through his clothes but failed to find it. On lifting his gaze to a coffee tree right above him, he saw a colony of agitated ants, and broke into a run. He stopped to catch his breath, and from close by he heard the furious fall of coffee seeds into baskets hooked to the coffee trees, while a singer spurred the workers on with her praise songs.

On tracing the source of the voice, it led him to Makemeh. Her voice was clear, almost sparkling, as she wove the names of the workers into her songs. Most of them were women. Their bare backs and their tough and tested shoulders glistened with sweat, as they filled baskets with coffee seeds which they then carried on their heads to a warehouse to be dried and cleaned. The women pulled frenziedly at the coffee seeds, their faces, their bared shoulders and breasts exposed to the assaults of killer ants whose bites sometimes occasioned fever or even death. They were in the grip of filling and emptying baskets with a dedication that rendered their faces the aspect of fierce competitors.

With the workers was an old man who looked on with an air of solemn importance. He was tall, dressed in a long gown, and with a trimmed goatee. On seeing William emerge from the cover of the bush and into a clearing, the old man stopped, and Makemeh did the same.

'So you followed me here,' she said.

She was sweating but sounded calm, her voice mirthful, full of delight and promises that made William's heart skip a beat.

'I wanted to know where you lived.'

Most of the workers had by then stopped and were watching William and Makemeh. A silence fell on the farm.

The man turned to his workers and roared at them:

'Go on with work or you'll have no lunch today. Who is this man?' he asked Makemeh.

'Mr Mawolo, meet my grandfather Boley.'

William extended his hand, but Boley ignored him and instead turned to his granddaughter with a stern gaze.

'Is he one of your suitors?'

Makemeh laughed.

'My grandfather is a jealous man, Mr Mawolo.'

'I came to repair the generator,' William said.

This piece of information brought a smile to Boley's face, and all of a sudden he was friendly and charming. 'Mr Mawolo, we truly hope that you are the man who would once and for all put a stop to the chronic malfunction of our generator. We are fed up with it.'

There was an aura of importance about him that even his working clothes could not conceal; his trimmed goatee with its dash of grey gave him an air of cultivated arrogance punctuated by his habitual toying with the edges of his gown.

'Where are you staying?'

'At the mansion.'

'That makes you the first person to ever occupy that house. You must be a very important man, Mr Mawolo.'

'The mansion was Old Kapu's idea.'

Boley nodded without a comment, as if he could read into William's answer the real purpose of his being in Wologizi. This was a man, William thought, one could easily get to dislike.

'It's lunch time,' Boley then shouted.

The workers came out of the coffee farm in rags, their sweaty faces lined with extreme fatigue, and they headed for the house where lunch awaited them. The house was a large, whitewashed affair which thundered at that hour of the day with the cry of children. Boley showed William to a sofa in a spacious living room and then disappeared into one of many rooms in the house, only to emerge later in a fresh, embroidered gown, ready for lunch. When William was about to join them, Boley stopped him. 'I'm sorry Mr Mawolo,' he said. 'I only feed those who work for me. That's the rule of this house.'

The tantalising smell of chicken cooked patiently in peanut sauce tormented William. His stomach churned, and despite the insult he craved to be part of those people squatted around the lunch in groups according to age and stature. On a dark-blue wall before him was a portrait of Boley right beside the president's, both large and impressive. The president looked young, full of vigour and promises, but a moustachioed Boley looked serious and with the rough edge of a hard-working farmer.

Makemeh came to William's rescue. She led him to a shaded corner of a courtyard with more than a dozen rooms looking out on it, and gave him a calabash of cold water. That afternoon, some boys had plucked a basket of mangoes from the trees that surrounded the house, two of which Makemeh decided to prepare for him. She covered the distance between him and the kitchen, which was part of the courtyard, aware of his intense gaze – felt it burning her nape even when she was not with him but in the kitchen, preparing the mangoes. Later she came out with chunks of the fresh fruit in a bowl. William attacked them, his hunger heightened by her presence.

'Is your grandfather always like that?'

'The townspeople call him "the Miser."'

'How was his relationship with your father?'

She seemed uncomfortable, and William thought that perhaps her father was a sensitive subject to her, his disappearance unbearable. She must be suffering, he thought, not knowing his whereabouts.

'You've started off on the wrong foot, Mr Mawolo.'

'No, I don't think so; you are the one who came to me.'

She pondered this for a while, and then decided to throw him a fragment from the past and see what he would do with it.

'It began with the storm, Mr Mawolo.'

Makemeh related the day her father came to see her on the rice field, which was part of the large farm, two years before his sudden disappearance. It was in the wake of a terrible storm that had spared most houses in Wologizi except her father's. The storm had carried away the entire corrugated iron roof, spreading the sheets scandalously on top of a tree behind his house. Before the disaster, Tetese had scraped a living by telling stories, an unrewarding profession, because he was not taken seriously by the townspeople, and as result he was often penniless. The incident with the roof only added to his misfortunes. Makemeh was pinching rice plants in the swampy soil, her feet knee-deep in the mud, the sun steadily burning her back, when she heard her father say, 'I came to see my daughter.'

Those words were directed at Boley, his father-in-law, and there was an unmistakable tone of anger in his voice. It was the first time she, Makemeh, had ever seen her father stand up to her grandfather. She had quickly crawled on all fours out of the swamp, anxious to reach her father before the situation escalated between the two men. On her face was a smile she was certain would calm him once he saw it.

'So you've heard about the roof,' Tetese said to her.

He seemed mollified by her presence, as if being with her made it possible to bear his misfortune with some pride. He would tell her that day that the one thing he regretted the most in life was not being able to bring her up, or to father her as was required of a man. Makemeh could see herself in him: the broad forehead, the impatient lips which moved constantly but would close whenever he became aware of them, as though it was a habit he loathed. And then there was his height: Tetese was as tall and as slender as she was. She noted, as if for the first time that day, the sharp difference in the colour of their skin, her father's as dark as soot, hers as bright as amber.

'What are you going to do now?' she'd asked.

Tetese had shrugged – 'I don't know.'

'And then,' William prompted. 'What happened then?'

'It was then that I suggested to my father to approach the Lebanese, Mr Mawolo. I told him that perhaps the Arab could help him with some corrugated-iron for his roof.'

'Why not your grandfather?'

'The two were not the best of friends,' she said and paused, gazing in the direction of the main door. 'My father always accused him of stealing the one person dearest to him – me.'

'What did the Lebanese do?'

'Why not ask the man himself?'

'How could a mere storyteller, who was not taken seriously by anyone, make it to the paramount chieftaincy?'

'I'm sorry, I cannot tell you this. My only suggestion to you is to begin your investigation with the Lebanese.'

She had a point, he thought. Perhaps it was better to hear out the Lebanese, and even though he doubted whether that would unravel the mystery of Tetese's disappearance he hoped it would lead him on the right track. The Lebanese, being a foreigner in that town, might know things that would be of some value to his investigation.

Makemeh promised to see him that afternoon. Then she stood up and led him through the house to the front door. The house was by then empty, most people having returned to work. For a while after she was gone, he paused before the closed door, vacillating between climbing down the hill or confronting her and ridding himself of the doubt that had gathered like phlegm in his throat. Though he'd been aware of every phase of their interaction, had he ended up yielding a part of himself to her? There was no sound of her footsteps on the other side of the door, which meant she was watching him. Was it to make sure he was gone and then gloat over the fact that henceforth he would be at her beck and call? What role was Makemeh actually playing?

Through a peephole Makemeh noted, as she watched him leave, that the stranger limped. Not even his lofty disposition, not even the expensive suit, could conceal the handicap. The stranger looked so solitary, so fragile before the storm of a series of events that had been unleashed before his arrival that she feared for him.

CHAPTER 5

The Lebanese, bald and pinched-faced, carried his potbelly like a load, every now and then pulling up his unbelted trousers as though to properly contain it. The moment he saw William, the Lebanese, who had cultivated the talent of weighing people up, quickly put him down as one of those men from the capital who were worth the attention only because they would not leave his shop without a packet of cigarettes, a bottle of strong drink, or a round of gossip about country girls whose docility titillated their imaginations. William indeed ordered a drink, sat on a bar stool, and leaning on the counter took slow sips at the bottle, turning it around on the counter in silence. The silence got on the Lebanese's nerves, and he decided to break it by inquiring from the stranger as to the purpose of his visit in Wologizi.

'I'm here to repair the generator.'
'Who asked you to do that?'
'Old Kapu.'
'It's about time.'
'I'm putting up at the mansion.'
'So, you are staying at the mansion?'

William nodded. 'Makemeh and a few women had cleaned it thoroughly. She told me she was Tetese's daughter,' he said, and as he gazed at the Lebanese he saw his face transform from a jovial one to one stricken by fear, which confounded him.

'Please know that I didn't have anything to do with it.'

'Anything to do with what?'

The Lebanese reached across the counter and grabbed him by the arms, and William noted that two fingers of his hands, the index and forefinger, were missing. 'With his disappearance.'

'What type of connection did you have with Tetese?'

'Connection? I wouldn't call it that. For years he sat in front of my shop. He was shunned everywhere, but I had no problem with him sitting there every day and wasting his time.'

The shop in which this event unfolded was located on the ground floor of a two-story building. From a once white but now yellow ceiling hung a fan which rattled in self-mockery, generating air that mingled with the smells of expired foodstuffs. Products of various kinds were stocked up in every corner: the walls covered with posters of voluptuous actresses all of whom were foreign. The master of that domain had arrived at Wologizi years before and had opened up the shop which, rumour had it but was never confirmed, was a joint venture involving Tetese's father-in-law, Boley, the man behind every successful enterprise in that town.

One day, the Lebanese had gone home and had returned with a tiny, sickly wife with whom he strolled hand in hand from one end of town to the other. Perhaps fed up with the drowsy monotony and solitude of a forest town, the wife had left him. Thereafter, dusk would often meet him standing in front of his shop, throwing lascivious glances at young women who laughed or mocked the nasal sound that accompanied his every word in the local language. He slept with some of them and lavished them with presents to silence them. The Arab had quickly aged. Time had shaved his head bald before he was even thirty, hence the nickname Baldhead, which had stuck like a leech to a body.

'One cannot help but wonder how it came about that an obscure storyteller could go on to hold the highest office in the entire forest region,' the Lebanese said. 'Look,' he leaned across the counter again, his large, bloodshot eyes fixed on William. 'I've lived among these people for more than thirty years. I've tolerated their unusual ways, I've seen strange things, but the most remarkable of them all is the case of Tetese, the well-known drunkard, the idler, the man of no consequence, the outsider who surprised us all with his paramount chieftaincy. This crowns them all.'

The Lebanese told William that the man who would later chop off his fingers without remorse had come to see him two years before. Heavy rain had caught up with Tetese, and when he entered the shop in large army boots which he claimed he had inherited from an uncle, he had left large patches of mud on the well swept-floor.

'Just because the storm has done such a wonderful job with your roof does not mean you have to dirty my floor, Tetese,' the Lebanese had said.

'I have a problem, Baldhead,' Tetese had said.

'What must I do to convince you people once and for all that my father, peace be upon him, had named me Gibril?'

'If you were to give me fifty pieces of zinc for a new roof I would make sure no one will ever call you Baldhead again,' he'd said, and the firm tone of his voice had thrown the Lebanese off his convivial balance.

'No way you could repay me.'

Tetese had tried by all means to persuade the Lebanese that he would get the money. And as he spoke, a mischievous smile had slowly crept over the Lebanese's face, and he had planted a kiss on Tetese's cheek.

'You could do me a favour in return for a new roof.'

A bewildered Tetese had nodded.

'You could tell me your best stories!'

'I could start right away.'

'I give you a week to prepare.'

Tetese had clicked the heels of his large army boots and had saluted the Lebanese, thrusting his chest forward and clasping his fingers. Meanwhile, the rain had gone on pouring in buckets, gurgling as it filled potholes and dragged along the town's refuse, depositing it in dark and seemingly impenetrable valleys.

'There are conditions attached to it though,' the Lebanese had warned. 'Once every week you come to me in clean clothes. There are to be no other audiences. The stories are told to me and only me.'

Tetese had nodded his consent.

As a token of good faith the Lebanese had given Tetese some pieces of corrugated iron for his roof.

'Then I watched him step in the rain, bearing the bunch of corrugated-iron on his head as cover, Mr Mawolo.'

'Did you live up to the bargain?'

'I should have if Tetese had done the same.'

'Was it then a question of revenge?' William pointed at the ghastly stumps.

The Lebanese, clearly disappointed, said, 'You must have been listening to rumours,' he said.

The day he came to see him, the Lebanese told William, Tetese was already a changed man. The man who often sat before his shop with his kora, waiting for a customer to praise his name to the skies, and who was often drunk, or humming a tune from one of his stories, was not the same Tetese with whom he'd closed that bargain.

'But the townspeople, from want of an explanation, have blamed me for triggering in him the man he later became.'

Every aspect of his chubby face, the anxiety that clouded it and the sweat that drenched it were all variations of a single longing to be believed. For the Lebanese was afraid that the townspeople might end up telling terrible lies to William about him, thereby turning the stranger against him. So, he hoped that by revealing more about Tetese he would cultivate William's trust. He went on to describe Tetese as a man of average height, light-skinned, almost yellow, but with patches of dark and grey spots strewn all over his body, a skin disease regarded by many in that forest region and beyond as peculiar to men with the extraordinary ability to be cruel.

William, who viewed this description as a desperate attempt on the part of the Lebanese to win him over, ignored it but listened on.

The Lebanese was emboldened by his silence. 'There was nothing special about his childhood,' he went on, 'except for his nickname, Tetese, the Torturer.' The nickname had stuck after Tetese had bound a childhood friend to a tree teeming with killer ants. This Tetese had gone away and had returned after years of absence bearing with him a bagful of stories, claiming he'd collected them all at various ports in the world. For a while, the townspeople, especially the young women, had taken to him. Tetese, to everyone's surprise, had ended up with one of them, the most beautiful girl in Wologizi.

'Boley's daughter,' William said.

The Lebanese nodded and fetched two bottles of soft drinks, one of which he gave to William, but it was lukewarm and only aggravated his thirst. The Lebanese was now convinced that William believed every word he'd uttered, but in fact William paid scant attention to these details. All he wanted was to get to the heart of the matter.

'They say Tetese vanished,' he said, 'and not of his own accord.'

The Lebanese agreed.

'That's what I was told.'

'By whom?'

William wanted to mention Makemeh but decided against it, but just before he could give a convincing lie, the Lebanese said: 'Tetese seems a victim, but don't underestimate him, Mr Mawolo. Never underestimate that man. Once he staged his own demise and everyone in Wologizi, including me, rushed out to celebrate his death, only to realise that he was alive and as healthy as a fish.'

The Lebanese left the counter and led William out to the front of the shop. Then he pointed at the horizon. 'You see those mountains, Mr Mawolo,' he said. 'Once upon a time when this region was plunged into internecine wars, they protected the town from invaders,' he said and paused to look William square in the face. 'But there was a less admirable aspect to them. Once a man found himself within their confines, it was difficult and sometimes impossible to escape them. So you see, the mountains function as haven as well as hell. Remember the duality, Mr Mawolo. '

'What have the mountains got to do with Tetese?'

'They could be a hiding place, a prison, or even a grave.'

William gaped at the mountains: they were huge, and their eternal presence, their majesty and the deep mysteries in which they were shrouded affected him. At that moment he was inclined to believe the Lebanese, but what if the man was embellishing these stories with the sole aim of persuading him with regard to his innocence? The Lebanese were a shrewd people. Most had come to the country penniless but had managed in a matter of a few years to control its economy, and this was achieved by whatever means. So perhaps the man was being untruthful to him for reasons of his own. Nevertheless, William thought that it was better to befriend him.

William patted the Lebanese warmly on the back and shook his hand before leaving him, a symbolic gesture, the Lebanese thought, that implied friendship and trust – the very things he'd hoped to gain from the stranger the moment his identity was revealed. 'That man is capable of protecting me,' the Lebanese told himself, not realising then that during all his years in Wologizi, it was the first time he had taken sides in anything.

CHAPTER 6

The setting sun framed the mountains that embraced a town that was often placid at noon but which, as the day fused into the night, gradually awoke. The mountains, knitted to the horizon on all sides of the town, were covered with sprawling canopies of verdant forests. The spectacle was so awesome that it could have been a scene from a mythical story, about an ancient town lying dormant within the confines of imposing mountains which, deep down their precipitous edges, harboured a secret it was reluctant to unveil.

William stopped to marvel at the craggy slopes that descended into deep valleys, and at minarets of mountaintops that pierced violet-red horizons. Behind him on the road, almost insignificant in relation to the mountains, he suddenly heard voices. He turned and saw women with bundles of goods on their heads returning from the market near the police station. They were conversing in cheerful voices as if the hectic hours at the market had only energised them. To a lewd remark from the men congregated under a tree at the roadside, drinking palm wine and conversing in amused voices about loves lost, conquered or about to be, the women responded with spirited jibes that only incited the men to throw more titillating phrases at them. For a while William was taken by the exuberant abandon and the contagious ease with which life unfolded in that place.

He resumed his walk. The checker players, on seeing him this time round, waved to him. 'So you are the one who came to deliver us from the darkness,' one of them said. They waved with enthusiasm to him, and he overheard them say he was a wonderful man.

Then it happened. On the very edge of the hill that led to the mansion, William almost trampled over a bundle of vine lying in the middle of the road. On its top, as if on display, were palm kernels, perhaps an offering to one of the gods, he thought. Slowly he approached the bundle out of curiosity and was about to touch it when it sprang loose like a trap, scattering the palm kernels, one of which hit his face, just missing an eye. In the shimmering air of that elapsing afternoon, William felt a sharp chill run down his spine. As he hurried away he saw threads of vine flanking the hill up to the mansion.

William feared no one, a disposition that had resulted from his interaction with some militiamen during his childhood. His aunt, the woman who had single-handedly brought him up after the death of his parents, would often claim that it was not the militiamen who had evicted them from their first home and thereby altered the course of their lives forever, 'but our fear of them, Moisoko.' Indeed, they had looked on helpless as the men had thrown their belongings on the street and then had burned them, cursing and swearing to boot. William and his aunt had been paralysed by fear, by the reputation that preceded the militia as a bunch of lawless men. Scarred forever by that incident, he had trained himself to conquer fear of men of whatever shade or build. In the process he had learned that the only way he could truly achieve his goal, this mastery of fear, was by attaining greater power than those who might threaten him. So he had joined the government, the source of power, and had risen through the ranks so quickly that he had been noticed by the president.

However, other fears remained, like the fear of the inexplicable, of loss of ability or of the lack of ambition, but the last two fell within the domain of his will power, which had never once failed him. In fact it had served him so well that at the Ministry of Interior, where he worked, everyone was convinced that one day he would become a minister. The inexplicable, like the incident with the palm kernels, troubled him.

Climbing up the hill, he hastened to the radio station to repair it but could not concentrate because his mind kept returning to the symbols on the road. What did they mean? Were they meant for him?

He longed to see Makemeh and to ask her about them, but she was not alone when she came that afternoon.

She was accompanied by the head of the militia, the policeman, whom William and Old Kapu had encountered that morning, marching with his men on the street. The policeman wore the same insolent look as before, and he was in his black and white uniform which, despite being worn out, seemed well ironed. The man looked healthy, and only his copper face, pinched here and there, betrayed his age. William was quick to note that between Makemeh and the policeman, an uneasy sort of relationship existed: the policeman appeared dismissive of Makemeh, but somehow she seemed to exercise a kind of power over him that had compelled him to follow her to see him.

'Corporal Gamla decided to come with me.'

The corporal grunted, as if he did not agree entirely with Makemeh, but extended his hand. The hand, though sweaty, was devoid of warmth, and this surprised William.

'I thought you would need his support and that of his militia if you are to make headway with your investigation,' she said.

William threw her a questioning look.

'There's no way you will get the townspeople to cooperate with you if you don't have the necessary force to back your words.'

He couldn't tell her how much he hated the militia, the men who had driven him and his aunt from his first home, only because a power greater than that of his aunt's had willed it. He remembered the days spent in search of a new home, penniless in a city of millions, and how finally the two had ended up in a shanty with a zinc house that rattled in the winds. He was afraid she wouldn't understand.

'I'll ask for help if I need it.'

'You need it now, Mr Mawolo.'

She made him feel redundant, which angered him. So, he left her and walked to the bench under the acacia tree. She must have noticed that he was upset because she followed him and set the bundle of dinner she had brought on the bench next to him. On opening it, the smell of potato-greens occupied the air, delicious, tantalising.

'I'm here for you, Mr Mawolo.'

There was no hint of coquetry in her voice, and it was this contradiction in her, this ability to astound him, that appealed to him. Suddenly he was aware of her proximity: she exuded the faint odour of a virgin bush, and she was so young and so full of vitality that he was momentarily assaulted with doubts as to his ability to influence her. This was new to him, because women were his territory.

'How many militiamen are there?' he asked.

'Fifty men or more,' she answered.

Meanwhile Corporal Gamla, who stood a distance away from them, grappled with a mixture of emotions. The moment he had seen William that morning with Old Kapu, the policeman had loathed and admired him at the same time. The stranger embodied the man he, Gamla, once was and should have continued to be, impeccably attired and with an enviable air of importance. It was the realisation of the loss of that irrecoverable past that had had the upper hand.

So he avoided the two, making as if he was going to pass water behind the mansion. He whistled as he disappeared from their sight. William began to discuss the corporal with Makemeh.

'They call him the town-crier,' she said.

'Why is that?'

'Because nothing ever escapes him.'

They could hear him whistling an old soldier song William knew from his school days. It was about a soldier who went on a murdering spree. When asked as to what incited him to commit those heinous crimes he answered that it was because he was given a gun.

William brought up the subject of the vines.

'Did you touch it?' Makemeh asked.

'It sprang loose in my face.'

Silence of an awkward sort lingered on for a while between the two, which was broken only when Old Kapu walked through the gate of the mansion. Corporal Gamla ceased his whistling and there was no sign of him. But Makemeh did not budge, even when William turned to her, imploring her with his gaze to leave. This was not the situation he had bargained for, not at that stage of the investigation. He did not want the old man to see him with Tetese's daughter, and when he stood up he saw himself moving away from Makemeh.

Old Kapu walked up to them in slow steps, as if it had cost him a great deal to climb up the hill. On reaching them, he coughed a couple of times to clear his throat, and then bowed his head as though to say something, but thought otherwise and kept silent.

With him were two of his wives, one of whom was Hawah Lombeh. She eyed William with such longing in her eyes that he was amazed; how could his fleeting action the other night have unleashed such a passion in her?

'We brought your food,' Old Kapu said.

The old man did not nod to Makemeh or acknowledge her presence in any way, and with his wives he entered the mansion. William was about to join them when Makemeh stopped him.

'The bundle of vine,' she whispered to him, 'is a symbol subject to various interpretations, both dark and colourful. They were perhaps not meant for your eyes unless you were the target.'

'The target of what?'

Cold sweat dropped down his armpits and on his feverish skin, and as he waited for Makemeh to go on he felt certain that Old Kapu was watching them from one of the windows.

'Perhaps of revenge or mere rage.'

'But I've only just arrived!'

'They know, Mr Mawolo.'

He knew it was true because he saw her beautiful face transform into hideous wrinkles of fear, as though all the while fear had been gathering like a storm in her and had now crashed across her calm and otherwise collected face.

'You have to act quickly.'

Then she headed for the gate. Although she left him as confused as prior to the revelation, he could not follow her because he thought that Old Kapu was still watching him from the windows. However, when he entered the mansion, he met the old man seated at the dining table with the disarming smile of a child spread across his face.

CHAPTER 7

The moment William entered the mansion, Old Kapu sent the two women away. On her way out, Hawah Lombeh paused at the door and her gaze rested on William, as if it contained a message for him, a gaze so intense it made him fidget in his seat. He knew it was unwise to encourage a woman who longed so much for him, because she might turn out to be unpredictable in her behaviour towards him, so he looked away. Hawah Lombeh and the other woman climbed down the stairs, the crunching sounds of their feet on the gravel receding into the distance.

The old man did not refer to the fact that he had seen Makemeh with William, but opted for long silences which were interrupted with a reference or two to the generator. The two were still playing the game begun the other day, but William decided to wait and see how events would unfold, and he vowed to remain alert. He knew he could not dine with the old man, not after what Makemeh had told him.

The two men sat at the dining table while the last sun rays glinted against the resplendent chandelier above it.

Old Kapu said: 'I would like to keep you company in this house for the time being, Mr Mawolo.' His words were slurred by the effect of the considerable amount of snuff on his tongue.

William suspected that the old man just wanted to keep an eye on him, just like the first time when the two met each other.

'I'm quite capable of being alone.'

'You might be bored in such a large house,' the old man insisted. 'You need the presence of someone like me, an old man, to entertain you with stories.'

William could not refuse, because on the surface and in the eyes of everyone he was still a guest, a repairman.

'Stories about what?' he challenged Old Kapu.

'About the town,' the old man said, rising to the challenge, and then after a short pause he said: 'How long do you think it would take you to repair the generator, Mr Mawolo?'

The old man knew exactly why William was in Wologizi, but still feigned ignorance, so William decided to do the same.

'Tomorrow I'll know more.'

Meanwhile the night had stolen up on them. In the darkness Old Kapu spat the residue of snuff on the floor but wiped it with his foot, as though he suddenly realised it was a concrete floor, not a dusty one. Later the lights came on. Insects of various kinds performed suicidal acrobatics around the chandelier; a large moth, singed by one of the bulbs of the chandelier, landed on the table before William. Its wings and antenna convulsed until it perished.

'The food is getting cold, Mr Mawolo. Since you are my guest, the saviour of Wologizi, for that's what everyone is calling you now, I want you to do me the honour of taking the first bite.'

'I dined a long while ago, Makemeh…;'

'You would be insulting me and throwing my hospitality back in my face if you refuse to take even a bite, Mr Mawolo.'

How much poison made up the sauce, William wondered.

'My stomach can't even bear a morsel.'

'You are my responsibility, Mr Mawolo, unless you tell me that I have fallen out of favour with you for no apparent reason.'

This game, this ability to pretend that nothing was amiss, began to upset William, and he was growing troubled in his seat.

'In fact I'll not take a bite until you do,' Old Kapu said, and he stood up to leave. 'You've spat in my face, Mr Mawolo.'

'I said no, old man! Or are you deaf?'

William was surprised by his own outburst, but relieved.

Old Kapu left his side of the table, walked up to him, and held him by the arms. 'It's an offence to anger a guest,' he said.

He fell on his knees before William, holding his feet, begging him in exaggerated phrases, refusing to stand up. The sight of the frail old man on his knees, a man who could have been his father or even his grandfather, compelled William to lay his hand on his head as a sign of forgiveness and to help him to his feet.

The old man had achieved his goal, but the food remained untouched and William was unable to strike up a conversation with him. After a while, Old Kapu retired to one of the bedrooms upstairs, from whence a crude symphony of his snores issued.

William, left alone to deal with the aftermath of the fallout, could not extricate himself from the clutches of the absurd thought that he was a target of someone's rage, nor that he had an enemy in the house in the person of the old man.

He longed for Makemeh, for her company and insight. Solitude compelled him to move to the window.

Wologizi lay in a deep slumber below him. The thought that within that darkness perforated with somnolent dots of light dwelled a force that protected a mystery, ready to vent its wrath on him, disturbed him. To cast off such uncanny thoughts he repeated to himself until he believed it that nothing would befall him.

The master bedroom to which he later retired owed its distinction solely to a life-size portrait on the wall. It was of the president. The octogenarian was a tobacco addict, with a pipe in all his portraits. Few ever saw him, and this had triggered wild rumours of his demise, which were refuted with another that claimed that he stayed alive by feeding on a concoction of bitter root-juices that would secure him a century and half of existence. Everything about him was veiled in a profound secrecy. Because the president identified himself with every city, town and village in the country and spoke all its languages fluently, every group claimed that he was one of their own and even invented outlandish stories to justify that claim.

The portrait dominated every aspect of the bedroom. The president must have been wrestling with a rage on the brink of an outburst when the picture was snapped, for his thick lips were pulled tight, his jaws were puffy and his eyes were boiling over with emotions that could only be interpreted as violent.

For years William had longed for an audience with the Old Man. This avuncular appellation had been adopted by the entire country the day the president swept to power while still in his thirties. Convinced like many others in the government that the Old Man closely followed his career, William had distinguished himself. Meanwhile he waited for fortune to smile on him. Then some days ago his dream had been realised with a single telephone call. It was from the Old Man himself. He was entrusting him with the task of journeying to the interior to inquire into Tetese's long silence. This request was not unusual because the Old Man was not unknown to maintain personal contacts with some paramount chiefs. That way, it was believed, he could keep his hold on the country.

William, who believed he'd been chosen on merit alone, promised not to disappoint the Old Man. On the phone, the Old Man's voice had been crisp, betraying no emotion. But at the end of the talk, just before hanging up, came a gentle laughter in which William thought he noted tenderness. Now he found himself smiling back at the portrait.

What made his heart sing with joy was the reality that he was one of the few to whom the Old Man had revealed a soft spot.

Mosquitoes buzzed about him, and he sought refuge under a net suspended above a king-sized bed, but the parasites clutched at it, waiting like hunting dogs at the mouth of a burrow. A sudden unease came over him when the lights went out. He sweated as if he'd come down with a bout of malaria. In the moonless darkness, an image, the cause of his discomfort, gradually rose before his mind's eye: it was Makemeh. She infected his mind with a feverish longing so tormenting that it denied him sleep. But as the hours wore on without a wink of sleep, the thought came to him that were she to materialise before him and slip out of her clothes, she might disappoint him. She might turn out not to be endowed with any particular beauty.

Yet, before him, he saw her smile which, as it spread on her face, took shape on his lips and teased his senses towards a climax that resulted in a brief but furious act of self-gratification.

In the darkness a hand reached out and touched him. He was glad Makemeh had come and had slipped into bed with him, naked and as desirable as his longing for her. He mounted her, and as he did so he recalled the first time he saw her standing at the door with the sunlight bathing her, her gaze locked with his own, a gaze so utterly consuming that he could not remember any woman staring at him with such intensity. How could he tell her then that her fate was inextricably linked with his own?

William explored the depths of her slender body, he caressed its firm curves, licked its salty surface, his imagination as sharp as though he were seeing her in broad daylight. And then Makemeh changed position, and her smell wafted to him. All of a sudden he realised that she did not smell of a fresh virgin bush, that her body was not as slender and as firm as he had supposed.

It took him a while to register the fact that in bed with him, clinging feverishly to him, was not Makemeh but Old Kapu's wife Hawah Lombeh. She had not left the mansion. She must have been in the room all the while, listening to his moans, and she must have got used to the darkness and had undoubtedly seen him panting with pleasure in bed. She repulsed him. So he wrenched himself furiously from her grasp. But Hawah Lombeh clutched at him, grabbing him around his waist. When he failed to wrestle himself away, he dragged her along the floor, kicking her to free himself.

'Please forgive me,' she pleaded.

How could he forgive her when all he felt was a fury of an unusual type raging in him, his whole body trembling to it?

'Don't make me hurt you,' he hissed.

He was conscious of Old Kapu in one of the rooms, perhaps eavesdropping on them. So he shoved her off him, quivering with a rage fuelled by the unbearable thought that she had seen him performing that most private of activities, the first time a woman had done so. It was this, more than anything else, which angered him.

Hawah Lombeh, as if to justify herself, said: 'All my life no man has ever touched me, and you did that last night. That is what brought me here; that is what led me to you.'

'But you are married!'

She was silent, and he could feel her hands reaching out to touch him in the darkness. There was hunger in those hands as they tried to overwhelm him with feelings to which he remained indifferent.

'Leave now,' he said in a hoarse whisper.

'I can tell you about Tetese and Old Kapu.'

She sounded desperate, he thought, a way of drawing his attention. Once again, she flung herself at him.

'Old Kapu is here, he might hear us. What do you think will happen if he knows what you are doing?' he said.

She was so close to him that he could see her eyes, and it seemed as he stared into them as if they reflected a torch of flame.

'Something happened in the past before Tetese was born…' she went on.

'That does not interest me,' he said. 'Leave me alone.'

But she refused, and he had the maddening urge to hurt her, which was exactly what he did. He grasped her arm, which was bony, cracking under his tight grasp, and tugged her to the door, while she resisted. He then threw her in the hallway, not caring whether her husband was awake.

He expected to hear her cry or the door to open, but he did not even hear her footsteps on the gravel. Hawah Lombeh left as silently as she had come. William berated himself for letting things to get that far with Hawah Lombeh. He cursed and swore while the night listened.

CHAPTER 8

Sleep continued to elude him that night. At a certain point he left the bed and paused before the president's portrait. In doing so he felt the Old Man's strength slipping into him and saw himself being armed with the certainty that despite all the odds he would bring the investigation to a successful close.

Suddenly, a voice interrupted him. It rose to a dirge similar to the one he had heard during his first night in Wologizi. Gradually it evolved into a single scream which came from down the hill, gathering pitch until it gobbled up the silence of the night. Then it abruptly ceased. Soon hurried footsteps populated the gravel ground of the house front. William could hear loud beating noises as of bodies clashing against each other, or as if someone was being tortured beyond imagination. Accompanying this clamour were anxious whispers, followed by the raucous laughter of a man, and then the high-pitched scream again, now a single sustained thrill, a heartrending squeal of such shattering impact that William felt his inside contract, as though his intestines would burst. The corrugated iron roof shook to the steady accumulation of sounds. The president's portrait fell over. The mosquito-net collapsed on William. The darkness around him became profound, and the room smelt of death and centuries-old ruins.

He hoped for dawn, and waited on his feet, tensed like a trap, and at one point when he could not stand it any more he bolted to the other room. But it was empty; Old Kapu had gone. He raced back to his room, locked it and waited for sunlight. When it came, he embraced its golden shafts that streamed through the chinks in the curtains. The light exorcised the experience of the night and emboldened him to leave the room and climb down to see whether the outside world had been affected by the incident. He had not left the room one minute when he was frozen in his steps by similar sounds from inside the building itself. It was a low incessant chant but of such harrowing intensity that, in its devastating effect on him, surpassed that of the night. Like a nocturnal frog that braves the daylight to escape the fangs of a venomous snake, William left the mansion and raced down the hill to the police station to see Corporal Gamla.

The policeman was sitting in a creaking chair, leaning against a peeling wall, his hands folded behind his nape. The foul odour of his sweaty armpits was oppressive in that tiny office of the police station.

The sun had risen with the heat, and because the office faced its path, bars of light poured through the glass window and fell on the corporal, soaking him in fetid sweat. On the wall behind him was a sepia portrait of the president with a pipe in his hand. The Old Man was flashing them a knowing smile, as if present in person.

There was a man with the corporal, the same man William had been with Makemeh on the street the other day. Cultivated mischief lingered about the man's lips, a leer of sorts that transformed his face into that of a conman. William hesitated in telling his story before the man, but Gamla assured him that a witness was necessary with such a serious case.

'But you are a government man, and I don't have to tell you all this,' he added. 'Carpenter Seleh can be trusted.'

Before William could begin his story, the carpenter told him that he was hard of hearing in one ear, so William should move to his left side. William ignored him and told his story.

'Carpenter Seleh,' the policeman said when William was finished. 'Perhaps you can help Mr Mawolo and me by telling us whether you heard any strange sound last night.'

The carpenter turned to William and laughed, revealing a gap between his upper front teeth, an imperfection that was however regarded by women of that forest region and beyond as the most attractive aspect of a man's face. William despised him.

'I slept uninterrupted last night, Chief.'

They were making fun of him. This carpenter, who knew little or nothing at all about him, was now calling him Chief, and William was offended because he believed it was a mocking title.

Corporal Gamla leaned forward. 'They call me the Town Crier simply because I'm often the first to know about every notable event in this town. I was one of the firsts to see you get off the bus two days ago, Chief. The whole of last night I was patrolling the town, like I do every night, in search of misfits who abound in this place.'

William realised that he had failed at imparting the full horror of his experience to the two men, so he decided to try again. But Corporal Gamla shook his head, saying that he would not pursue the case if the Chief did not come up with a witness. William stared the policeman square in the face and told him what had been nagging at him since last night.

'It must have been the work of the Poro,' he said.

William had taken the two men by surprise, so their first reaction was that of stunned silence. Then the carpenter laughed.

'You mean the Poro secret society?' he asked. 'You know as well as I do that the role of the Poro nowadays is merely ceremonial.'

'The ancient tradition is dead,' the corporal said. 'Perhaps where you come from. . . ' He was interrupted by a strangled howl from a nearby room. William hurried to its source, having decided to play the role of their 'Chief'. Then he saw huddled in a corner, hands crowded about his chest, his face wrinkled with anxiety, the beautiful young man he had encountered the day he stepped off the bus.

In that environment – which reeked of faeces and urine – the young man had lost nothing of his beauty.

'Why are you shouting like that?'

'There are forces out to suffocate me, sir,' he said in a voice choked with fear, his eyes dilated as though he'd been confronted with something terrible in that cell.

'What forces?' William asked.

'Look around you, sir, they are everywhere.'

William, surprised to learn that the young man he had assumed was deaf when he first met him the other day could talk, was silent.

'Beware of Gamla and the carpenter, sir.'

That the corporal was standing behind William escaped the young man. On hearing him, the corporal shoved William aside, opened the cell, stepped in and locked it behind him. Using a baton fashioned out of the hardest tree in that forest region, he confronted the boy. The blows fell like the relentless strikes of a woodcutter. Every attempt on the young man's part to dodge the blows and his heartrending cries only inflamed Gamla. Every time he fell, Gamla would gather him up and flatten him against the damp wall and begin anew, until the young man's cries turned into a surrendered silence. Only the dull thudding of baton against flesh was heard now.

Meanwhile William had grown agitated. 'Stop it,' he called repeatedly, but the policeman went on. So William rushed to the office and took the president's portrait, flashing it before the policeman.

'I represent the Old Man,' he shouted.

The effect was tremendous. The corporal jumped to attention and saluted him with a loud click of his boots, exactly as William had expected. Though aware of his role as a law-enforcement officer, Corporal Gamla worshipped the mysterious, the powerful. That was why he decided to obey the stranger, the Old Man's representative.

'So you are not here to repair our generator, Chief,' the carpenter said. 'Then you've come to the right place. There's no town in the world as full of liars as Wologizi; a place where you would meet a man tapping palm wine only to tell you he's cutting firewood.'

'Shut up,' William snapped, and turning to the policeman he said with determination in his voice: 'Unlock the door, Corporal.'

William entered and gathered the young man in his arms. And as he helped him to his feet, he thought he saw profound gratitude in his eyes and something else he could not place.

'You have to admit, Chief,' the carpenter said, 'that a beauty such as his is rare even among women. Just look at him. I thought so once upon a time, but he's a common thief.'

'What do you mean?'

'Why do you think he's here?'

'The young man is the carpenter's houseboy, Chief,' corporal Gamla said. 'I caught him last night sneaking away with one of his boss's treasured possessions.'

'My most treasured possession, Chief,' the carpenter said. 'Over the years I've designed many things for many wealthy people, and I've furnished hundreds of houses including our "mansion". But my most treasured and most beloved work of them all is this sculpture.'

The sculpture, which lay on the table, was of a hand, slender and smooth as marble. William had to own that it was of an extraordinary craftsmanship: the wrist was designed in the form of a plaited head of a woman. Evidently it had taken the carpenter a lot of time and effort to carve the sculpture into an almost natural form.

William turned to the youth for some kind of explanation, a defence of sorts, but he was silent, his gaze conveying nothing.

'Just let him be,' he finally told the two men.

Carpenter Seleh broke into a raucous laughter. As his voice filled the small space of the room William thought he had heard it somewhere else, and then it struck him: the laugh was similar to the one he had heard last night. The carpenter had been there.

'You don't know the rules that govern this town, Chief,' the carpenter said, facing William, as if blocking his way out.

The two men, the carpenter and William, were of the same height, but while the carpenter was broad-built, intimidating in his elegance, William was sinewy but armed with the conviction that he could thrash the carpenter in a fight. The carpenter seemed taller, however, and every time he addressed William he emphasised this difference by seeming to stare down at him. This enraged William.

So he drew himself to his full height.

'I say: release him,' he ordered.

Corporal Gamla obeyed without reluctance. The young man, who until then had not been sure that William would have the upper hand, fled out of the police station as if he was being chased.

'Whoever breaks the law must be punished, Chief. Someone who works for you and betrays your trust deserves the prison. You are making an enemy of me, Chief, and no one can afford to make an enemy of Seleh because I'm a difficult man.'

'You were there last night, weren't you?'

'What are you talking about, Chief?'

'The sounds, last night.'

'You must have been dreaming.'

Stung by this remark, William charged at the carpenter but the man dodged him. The two men faced each other. Everything happened so quickly that William could only recall a sharp tool slashing across his face. The world whirled about him and he fell with a heavy thud. Later he awoke to find himself in the Lebanese's shop, stretched out on a collapsible chair, with the man bandaging his wound. Corporal Gamla looked on from a prudent distance.

Whatever it was, the tool had cut just under the surface of William's skin around his chin, but blood still poured out of him. He could not believe he had lost so much blood. It was everywhere: on his shirt and trousers, and on the floor.

'Baldhead is the only one in Wologizi with a first aid kit, Chief,' Corporal Gamla said. 'And the hospital is miles away.'

The Lebanese nodded.

'They bring their sick to me, and not only do I sell them my products but I doctor them as well – imagine that, Chief.'

The Lebanese held him down and tended with an unusual zeal to the wound. Even after bandaging the wound, he fussed about him. Fed up with him, William asked him to fetch him some fresh clothes. He was still dizzy when he sat up to put them on. Touching the bandaged chin, he realised that the forest town had marked him forever.

Meanwhile the Lebanese ranted on about the danger that was the carpenter. 'Over the years carpenter Seleh has managed to make an enemy of everyone in this town.'

'Don't listen to him, Chief,' the corporal said.

The presence of William, whom the corporal reverently addressed as "Chief", emboldened the Lebanese, and so he said, 'Everyone knows that you worship the carpenter.'

'You are doing the same thing now, Baldhead.'

'What do you mean?'

'You are befriending the Chief to save your skin.'

The Lebanese hurled vituperative accusations at the policeman. He told William that the corporal had once connived with the carpenter to oust Old Kapu from the chieftaincy.

The corporal agreed that their action had been wrong, but that it could only be explained in relation to Tetese, the man who had triggered it all. Old Kapu, the town chief, had failed to intervene when Tetese had mistreated the townspeople.

'Tetese was a sham, Chief,' he concluded. 'Everything he ever did, 'the storyteller he claimed to be and the bargain he struck with Baldhead were all a sham.'

The Lebanese did not interrupt him, and when William spoke he felt the pain from his wound: 'How did you know that?'

Corporal Gamla answered that there were a host of instances to prove his point, but he chose to refer to the night Tetese arrived at the Lebanese's shop to tell his stories. Out of obligation to uphold the law and the wish to cooperate, he was about to tell Mr Mawolo what perhaps had been the turning point in the history of Wologizi.

CHAPTER 9

It was a moonles night, Corporal Gamla recalled, and the darkness was so absolute that houses were mistaken for anthills. Word had reached the corporal, as it had everyone else in Wologizi, that the bald Lebanese had struck a bargain with Tetese, but no one could trace the source of the rumour which seemed to have always existed but was only then manifesting itself. It was as if the whole of Wologizi had come out to listen to Tetese.

At first the Lebanese had been hostile to the point of revulsion at the presence of such a large crowd in his shop. 'You will dirty my floor and purchase nothing, you bunch of riffraff,' he had shouted at the people, but in the end had succumbed to the inevitable: he could not chase them away.

To prepare for the night, the Lebanese had filled up his generator with enough gasoline because there was a power cut that night. He came down to join the crowd, wearing an ivory-white caftan lined at the edges with golden filigree, his grey moustache dyed jet-black, his bald head smoothed over with lotion.

Earlier that week some people had seen Tetese rehearsing the stories as he strolled the streets. He had told them that he intended the stories to complement each other, to be situated in different periods in Wologizi's past, with the lives of townspeople, their secrets, shames and loves, woven together in a single tapestry.

Old Kapu, who graced the evening with his frail presence and was allocated a place befitting a chief, right at the head of the seated and standing crowd, would often claim that he was not really interested in Tetese or his stories: 'I was merely there to witness him make a fool of himself.' Even Tetese's father-in-law, Boley, was present that night. But on more than one occasion he was reported to have said, as if to justify his presence: 'I was on my way to persuade my daughter that it was in her best interest and in the interest of Makemeh to once and for all divorce that fool, when I saw the crowd.'

Tetese was the last to enter the shop. The crowd watched him edge his way to a spot in the middle of a circle of people. Many would recall later that he had been wearing black trousers and a faded red shirt which he had claimed he had bought at a port somewhere in the world. 'Of course he was just showing off, Chief,' the corporal told William, 'because I had seen him purchase that very shirt at the local market.'

Something was amiss, for no sooner had Tetese begun than he broke into a fit of coughing that shook his body down to his toes. As the crowd looked on he struggled but failed to tell his stories. His eyes were bloodshot, his lips tremulous, and his breath heavily stale – characteristics of a seasoned drunkard. Minutes after he'd started telling his story he gave up and left the shop. The crowd began to boo him as he edged his way through a throng of people.

It was raining and the night was as dark as pitch, but now and then lightning would sketch irregular stripes against the firmament. These stripes of light had guided Tetese on his way to his home, part of which he had roofed with the corrugated iron the Lebanese had given him a week before.

The crowd grew restless. It began to blame the Lebanese for Tetese's failure to live up to the bargain. The Lebanese, afraid that their anger might boil over into violence and he might end up losing some of his products, tried to calm the crowd down. But after a while Tetese fortunately showed, but this time he was not alone.

Corporal Gamla saw him and his wife emerge out of the cover of darkness and come into the light of the shop. Meanwhile, the crowd had been busy recalling various episodes from his life. Someone whose name the corporal could not recall now had reminded the mirthful crowd of a particular period in Tetese's childhood when he had locked a cat in a box and had torched it. Moreover, the fire which had once burned down the hut which Tetese had shared with his mother had been ignited by him. For, as the entire community struggled to put out the fire and save the mother caught in the flames, the child Tetese had stood under a tree, bearing a serene expression on his face. Such was Tetese as a child.

The crowd roared with laughter when it saw Tetese being led into its midst by his wife. She was a giant of a woman, the corporal told William, big-boned and taller, much taller than her husband. It was rumoured and even ascertained by some, including the corporal himself, that she thrashed him in every domestic squabble. She entered with her husband, whose arms were tied behind him, and she was so close to him that her breath poured down his cheek as she said: 'You are going to tell those stories tonight, Tetese. Especially those ones with which you once beguiled me into falling in love with you, thereby defying my father and the expectation of the town. Despite your alcoholism, I chose to stick with you. Finally, when commissioned to do what you've always claimed to be best at, telling stories, you feign failure. I don't want to hear it.' And she forced him to sit down.

'No one saw what I then saw then, Chief,' the corporal told William with conviction. 'No one but me saw those flames. And that smile, as though Tetese was mocking the townspeople, mocking us for our failure to see through the mask he had worn for years: the mask of a failure, the mask of a man subjugated by his wife.'

It was at this point that corporal Gamla turned to the Lebanese, as if to inquire whether he wanted to add something, or to contradict him, but the Lebanese was silent, so the corporal went on.

'That night, Tetese told us his stories, Chief. Stories full of violence and internecine conflicts which I don't have the stomach to repeat. The next day he vanished into thin air.'

This account baffled William. Tetese had been portrayed as a caring father by his daughter, but from what he had heard from the Lebanese and the corporal, he was a fool and a failure. William wondered which of the portraits was authentic.

'You sound as if he was more than one person, Corporal,' he said.

'But that's what he is and more, Chief,' the Lebanese said, joining the conversation. 'He could surprise us this very minute with a sudden appearance, and we would be left as dumbfounded as before. The man is and remains a deep mystery, Chief.'

In this the two men seemed to agree. But William was not satisfied. He was missing an aspect of Tetese, a deeper understanding of the man and his motives, especially how he had made it from a mere failure to paramount chieftaincy, the highest post in the forest region. And then there was the problem of the auditory phenomenon at night and the question whether it had to do with Tetese.

He turned to the Lebanese. 'Were you disturbed out of your sleep last night by strange sounds?' he asked.

'You are going on again about the Poro, Chief,' the corporal said. The Lebanese did not answer. His gaze moved from William to Gamla, and it was evident that he was hiding something.

'Corporal,' William called the policeman.

Corporal Gamla drew himself to full attention with an exaggerated click of his army boots, and he saluted.

'Yes, Chief,' he boomed.

'Assemble the militia at once. We are going to pay Old Kapu a visit,' he said and walked out of the shop.

The Lebanese was bewildered by the sudden turn of events. He rushed after a man he had hoped to befriend, but to no avail. As he stood before his shop, he watched William walk with proud steps, as if the very ground beneath his feet belonged to him.

CHAPTER 10

Corporal Gamla was right, William thought as he waited on the roadside for the policeman to return with the militia. What he, William, had experienced the other night could not be the work of the Poro. The incident was too extraordinary to be ascribed to that secret society that had survived for centuries in his part of the world but that nowadays 'only had a ceremonial function,' as the carpenter had aptly put it.

William was himself an initiate. Years ago, as a young man, he had been taught the basic principles of the Poro with the goal of crossing over from childhood to adulthood, or, in other words, being reborn. Rebirth, the cleansing of a man to prepare him for the hard world, was the essence of the Poro. But what he remembered foremost from that ephemeral period were not the archaic and elaborate rituals performed as a prerequisite to being accepted as a full-fledged member of the society, but the sight of a naked woman spread out on a bamboo bed. She had been employed to teach the initiates the rudiments of sex.

It was night. He sat with a bunch of frightened boys before a hut, all silent and anticipatory. Each initiate would enter upon the woman and emerge without sharing his experience, as if what occurred in that hut forbade speech. Then it was his turn. On pushing open the reed-door of the hut, he could not see her at first because her charcoal hue had blended with the darkness. Then his eyes became accustomed to the dark. He saw her stretched out in bed, a very big woman, her knees slightly parted. She flashed him the whiteness in her eyes, and although she breathed heavily, a deep but regular rise and fall of breath that betrayed fatigue, her gaze was indifferent. She gestured to him, and he approached with some hesitation. Only then did he catch a smell, not of sex because he was yet to know how it smelled, but of sweat and of fear, and of the cloak of innocence abandoned by others in that room. She reached for his member, and he shivered only to begin to feel a strange but pleasant sensation between his legs, followed by a sudden, gratifying release.

Whatever he had experienced last night must be the work of some men in Wologizi who wanted to scare him off. Old Kapu would know more about it, he thought, and was determined to get it out of him.

The militia finally showed up, marching to the raspy voice of the policeman. The men followed William without questioning his motives, because he represented a power beyond their grasp. Therefore he needed no introduction or a rousing speech of any kind, for an allusion to that power alone in whatever way, even in his silence, especially in his silence, was enough to convince them of his authority. The men had become, like their commander, his private army.

How he wished then that his aunt was there to see him leading these militiamen, this group of people who had put an end to his idyllic life in his town of birth. She would have applauded him, heaved a sigh of relief, and sung his praises. It was not the joy or the satisfaction that he'd had his revenge that welled up in him, but a more powerful feeling: the reality that he had evolved from a boy whose future was once confined to a small town to a man who commanded an army.

Wologizi at that hour of the day was shrouded in a shimmering haze as after a forest fire, the skies a panoply of dark clouds which seemed to have merged with the haze. Somewhere a stray dog broke out into a fit of barking. Others followed, and the forest town was suddenly overwhelmed with howls. Clouds of dust swept across the streets, whispering blasphemies, gathering force until they joined with the skies. Another gust of wind rose hard on the heels of the first, an impetuous wind of dust which hit the men flush in their faces, including William.

The incident was witnessed by none other than Hawah Lombeh. She was sitting with a group of old men under the breadfruit tree. On seeing William, she rushed over to him to help dust him down. What was a woman doing in the midst of such old men, William wondered.

In daylight, Hawah Lombeh seemed surer of herself than the pleading woman of last night. She moved her rough hands across his clothes and face with an effusive tenderness that got on his nerves. She admonished him: 'Why let the dust stain those nice clothes of yours?' What was it that prevented him from stopping her? He loved women, loved them with all his heart, because they were an extension of his existence, the group with whom he felt safe, secure and in his element, the ones in whose world he was brought up, thanks to his old aunt. Hawah Lombeh was an exception, however.

Gazing at her, the cracks between her lips stained with dried blood, her face scarred with hardship, William berated himself for falling into the trap she had obviously set for him.

The old men, the militia and Corporal Gamla looked in amusement, while Hawah Lombeh fired questions at him.

'Why is your face bandaged? Did you fall? Tell me!' Her whole face was deeply furrowed with concern. She added slowly so that only William could hear her: 'You should take better care of yourself in this town, otherwise incidents much worse than the one with the wind of dust or the fight with the carpenter might befall you.'

Because he remained silent, she opened her mouth as if to say something. He thought he heard her whisper Makemeh's name but was not sure, and so he asked what she'd said.

'Why the militiamen?' she asked, now loudly.

She sounded like his old aunt, concerned about his well-being, adroitly playing the maternal role. That was the problem with some women, he thought, assuming roles not cut out for them.

'I'm going to meet your husband.'

He said it to spite her.

'You don't need the militia for that. What you need is to use your senses properly in this town, to open your eyes.'

'I need the militia to protect me.'

'But there are things the militia cannot help you with.'

'I should be the judge of that.'

'What are you going to do with my husband?'

'You'll see,' he said.

'Please don't hurt him.'

This made him laugh, for why should she care whether a husband who obviously did not love her and whom she had betrayed the other night was hurt or not? He left her and called the militia to follow him. Corporal Gamla seconded his order by shouting angrily at the men, who formed a single file behind them. Hawah Lombeh followed closely at the rear. At one point he turned to her with a piercing gaze that rooted her to the ground, and she did not move until

William and his men reached her husband's home. Then she broke into a run in another direction. The old men resting under the breadfruit tree gaped at her, bewildered by her strange behaviour.

Old Kapu's compound was cloaked in a peculiar silence, which caused William and his men to stop and listen for a while, as though something terrible was about to happen, before he mounted a crude flight of steps to the veranda and went through the long corridor to the rear of the house where he met some members of the household.

'Old Kapu has taken ill,' a woman said.

The old man had left the mansion at dawn and had come in trembling with fever. 'He cannot see you now,' she added.

From one of the rooms, as if to confirm her words, a grunt issued from someone who seemed in the throes of death. This sent some women rushing into the room only to emerge screaming, their hands on their heads in a gesture of grief, their raucous cries throwing the entire household into panic. William entered and met Old Kapu spread out on a mat with various medicines scattered about him, including some tablets and herbs. Two women were attending to him. One was soaking a piece of cloth in warm water and spreading it across the length of his back, and the other was feeding him a herbal concoction.

'So you've come,' the old man said.

Old Kapu turned around on his back and gestured to a chair, which one of the women fetched. He asked William to take a seat.

'My backache has returned,' Old Kapu grunted, and he looked so frail that William thought that another jolt of pain would be enough to dispatch him to the other world. 'When the pain returned last night I left because I did not want to disturb your sleep,' he said, gritting his teeth, and after a while he asked: 'Have you had your breakfast?'

William shook his head.

'Ask the women to prepare some food for you. A hungry guest is a curse to a household,' he said, breaking into a fit of coughing.

William decided to leave.

'Stay a bit longer and keep me company.'

'You need rest,' William insisted.

The room stank of pungent herbs, and of impending death. On leaving it, William took in a long breath of fresh air, certain that the old man would not survive the day. He crossed the corridor and was almost outside when he heard a voice say – 'Fetch me my breakfast. That Mawolo man does not realise he's 'playing with fire."

It was Old Kapu. William could hardly believe his ears. Was the old man feigning his illness? But why? And what did he mean by playing with fire? If the old man thought he was a fool, then he would prove him wrong. He entered the room again, this time accompanied by his men, to confront the old man and compel the truth out of him.

Old Kapu seemed not in the least surprised to see him.

'So, Mr Mawolo, this time you chose to return with the militia. You remind me of someone I knew and loved once upon a time.'

'You lied to me, old man!'

'You are the one who came to us claiming you were just a passer-by. Now you confront me with the militia.'

Old Kapu sat up on the mat, and dismissed the women with a sucking of his toothless mouth, followed by a practised hiss.

'When did you find out why I had come to Wologizi?'

'Does it matter?' Old Kapu asked.

'Tell me!'

'The first time I saw you.'

'Tell me everything.'

'You wouldn't believe me if I told you that I loved Tetese, that I was one of the few in Wologizi who actually helped him on several occasions, even when I knew he was a hopeless case.'

'Tell me about his disappearance. What happened?'

'We thought you would come with an answer. The last time Tetese disappeared he returned as a paramount chief. Who knows, perhaps the next time he returns it will be as a minister.'

'Quit this pretence, old man!'

William approached the old man and loomed large over him, so that the old man cringed, saying, 'The only episode I can share with you, Mr Mawolo, is Tetese's visit to me in the aftermath of the storm. Or the night at the Lebanese's shop.'

'I'm not interested in that episode, old man.'

But Old Kapu had already begun, and William, exasperated with him, was about to leave when the old man said, 'Tetese was shorter than me, Mr Mawolo.'

'But I was told that Tetese was tall.'

'Lies, Mr Mawolo. Look, whenever he stood beside me, I could see the top of his head which had traces of baldness. That's how tall our storyteller was, Mr Mawolo. But you are disturbing the flow of the story, and you'll end up confusing me. Where was I? Yes, Tetese came to see me after the storm, and I said, looking him square in the eyes: "Tell me what it is you want from me? A new house?" '

'You are being sarcastic, Old Kapu,' Tetese had said.

'What I'm saying is true. You've never done a day's work your entire life. And just after the storm has done such an admirable job with your roof you come to me – it's no coincidence.'

'I need a loan for a new roof.'

Old Kapu had thrown a conspiratorial glance about him but had seen no one, except a he-goat tethered to a tree. Nevertheless he'd leaned towards Tetese and had whispered: 'Son, don't tell anyone what I'm about to say. For years now I've not been paid a cent for my work as chief of Wologizi. If you were to tell me how I survive with so many obligations, including feeding a household full of good- for- nothing women, I'll build you a house of your choice, with roof and all.'

Only then did the old man become aware of the transformation in Tetese. From a man who had once embodied indolence itself, he had turned into one who now pulled himself together and said dryly, 'You'll pay for your refusal, old man.'

'I laughed at him, Mr Mawolo, because I could not imagine him being anything else than what he already was, a complete failure.'

'Why, of all people, did Tetese approach you?'

'Because I'm soft-hearted, Mr Mawolo, a fool.'

'That could not be the only reason.'

For the first time Old Kapu looked perplexed and then a helpless smile appeared on his face. 'A man like you, Mr Mawolo,' he said, shaking his head, 'always outsmarts people like us who live in such a backward place like Wologizi. You have your charms as assets, and your ability to turn any woman's head. Tell me who whispered this secret into your ears, a woman?'

William heard his men laughing in the back.

'I bet it was a woman, perhaps one of my women. You see, Mr Mawolo, my curse, the burden I must carry to the end of my days, is my wrong choice of women.'

The allusion to Hawah Lombeh and the men's laughter angered William so much that his eyes took on a menacing aspect.

'You will tell me what happened to Tetese.'

'There's nothing you can do to me which has not been done tenfold to me in the past, Mr Mawolo. Here I am, ready.'

'We'll see, old man.'

William went out of the room and gave a speech to his militia, which he felt was necessary at that moment. He wanted them to go beyond their mere support for him and believe in him like he believed in the Old Man. 'It's important that you carry out my orders because they come directly from the Old Man himself,' he said, and the men nodded, just as he'd anticipated. 'If you back me, I'll make sure that each one of you is incorporated in the regular army and paid monthly, and on time. I give you my word.'

The short speech roused the men, and in their eyes he could see the eagerness to please him. He gave an order to two of them to cart Old Kapu off to the town hall where he would join them later.

'Corporal,' he turned to Gamla. 'I want you and the rest of the men to gather the townspeople in the town hall. I want to know what happened to Tetese before sunset. Now move, Corporal.'

The sight of the militia descending on the town to carry out his order suddenly awoke in William an acute awareness of his own capabilities. Never before, in all his life, had he felt such power over men, but what was much more profound than this awareness was the certainty that soon Wologizi would yield to him and reveal the truth. This power, coupled with this certainty, so overwhelmed him that he felt dizzy.

William felt alive as never before.

CHAPTER 11

Because he had to do something to master the passion that was ebbing and flowing in him at the mere anticipation of soon standing before the townspeople in the hall, William went up to the mansion to repair the radio. There he met Makemeh. On seeing her, he caught his breath, thinking: 'So, she will be there to witness it all, to see me in action.' She was sitting on a wooden bench under the acacia tree, in a yellow blazer and a long, black pleated skirt, her hands resting on the bench, her arms curled up against her sides. Splotches of sunlight that had escaped the foliage bathed her, giving her skin the black-and -white aspects of an initiate. Makemeh was relishing the cool shade, keenly aware of the power she exercised over the man who, instead of entering the radio station to repair it, hurried towards her. The serenity about her, her utter composure complemented in every way what he felt at that moment: a master of his own destiny.

Makemeh then presented him with a smile that leaped across the distance between them and landed on the tip of his lips, forcing them to part into a similar expression.

She had brought him some oranges. Out of gratitude or perhaps surrender to the dictate of the moment, he reached out but fell short of touching her arms. Those long slender arms, he noted, were strewn with fine hair. They said of hairy women, he thought as he sat beside her, that their passion was unbounded. Most of her fingernails were broken, her palms craggy, perhaps from hard work. She peeled an orange for him in a tiny thread that did not break until she was finished. She watched him suck the juice out of the orange.

Silence offered the two of them some precious moments to appraise the unspoken feeling that had gradually awoken in them, especially in William, and he regretted when she broke it.

'Something seems to bother you, Mr Mawolo.'

'What do you mean?'

'You seem afraid of me.'

Her words were like a stone from a catapult that hit him hard where it hurt most, and he heard himself saying: 'I'm not afraid of women, I respect them, and in fact I was brought up by one.'

He told her that his aunt had brought him up single-handedly after the death of his parents in a car crash. On leaving the village where the local militia had thrown them out of their home, the two had ended up in the capital in a shanty house on the edge of a cliff, the most dingy place in the entire city. There she taught him to value education, even though she herself was an illiterate.

Strange, he thought now, that he was pouring out his heart to the daughter of a man at the centre of a mystery. From where had this sudden compulsion emerged? He turned to her. The harshness of life in a forest town had not broken her. In fact there was no trace on her face to indicate that she'd ever endured hardship. She carried the worries of her father's disappearance deep in her heart.

He had had many women in the past, had relished the attention they lavished on him, and with every woman, except for a few, he felt he owed it to himself to love her properly, to shower her with attention, because a woman on her own had brought him up.

Makemeh was unlike any of them, unlike Hawah Lombeh, that agitated woman who always got on his nerves. Tetese's daughter remained a mystery, fascinating but incomprehensible.

She listened to him now, her gaze intent on him. Such attentiveness brought out the deepest compassion in him, and he felt he could love her as he'd never loved any woman before.

'What's bothering you then?'

He told her about his fight with the carpenter, about the bandaged wound, brushing her worries aside by saying boldly, 'I'll see to it that he gets his due.'

She eyed him steadily, and in those eyes he noted the fervent wish for him to carry out his threat to the letter.

'What if the town took his side?' she asked.

'Then we'll teach the town a lesson!'

He said it to please her, but he realised that men in his position should not to utter such words. What he'd just done emphasised his inability to contain himself in her presence. It irritated him because it was so unlike him. But why was she bent on punishing the carpenter, he wondered. Henceforth, he decided, he would have to exclude her from the investigation, if he wanted to remain in charge.

Then he recounted the night's incident, leaving out the episode with Hawa Lombeh. Makemeh was silent, but he saw how fear clouded her face, and so he so changed the subject.

'I must radio the capital at once. By now they must be eager to know how much progress I've made,' he said.

'I want to see you do it.' She drew closer to him, so that their hands nearly touched, and when they entered the radio station she took a seat on a bench beside a wooden pole which seemed the only force that held together what was otherwise a dilapidated building. The windows were broken. There were cracks in the walls, part of which had been darkened by smoke, as if the house had once been a kitchen. In a gloomier part of the room, covered in spider webs but still visible, was the Old Man's portrait, his face partly veiled by smoke from his pipe, betraying no emotion whatsoever.

Despite all Wiliam's efforts at repairing it, the radio kept hissing and crackling, or he would receive a constant buzz that grated on his nerves. The setbacks of the past days, combined with the rustle of Makemeh's skirt, indicating her impatience, steered him towards an outburst. Then he saw it. Sands had been poured into the headset, the obvious work of saboteurs. The radio was beyond repair. He banged the headset on the floor with a force that shattered it to pieces. He left the station trembling with rage, until he felt Makemeh's touch, a soft pleasant touch that felt almost like a caress.

She led him to the mansion, and once inside, he felt at ease. He watched her moving about the living room, admiring a cupboard with a collection of porcelains and caressing an armchair with the country's flag carved on its back, one of the carpenter's most accomplished works. Following her with his eyes, he imagined what it would feel like holding her in his arms, leading her upstairs and spreading her out on that king-size bed, and then, with a practised deftness, leaving her panting afterward. So palpable was this daydream that when he snapped out of it he was shocked to see Makemeh standing behind the carpenter's work, her entire disposition seeming to defy that vision.

Later, as he led her out of the gates and down the hill towards the town hall, he wrestled with the implication of her gesture. Was she conveying a message or a warning to him? The two were facing the full glare of the sun, which captured the deep dark of his face and set Makemeh's skin at glow. Her nose quivered with anticipation, her neck was beaded with sweat, her breath calm but with a nervous edge to it, which he interpreted as her impatience to see him in action.

The two militiamen who had accompanied Old Kapu to the town hall had stationed themselves at the bottom of the worn-out steps that led to the main entrance. William told them to wait outside until the rest of the townspeople were present. Then he led Makemeh to the platform. Somewhere on the ceiling and around the main entrance lizards frolicked about, breaking into noisy scuffles which ended with one alighting before the two. The lizard acknowledged them with a nod before climbing the perforated wall of the hall and disappearing out of sight.

He gazed down at her necklace, a set of crude beads that had been collected in the forests, and then he reached for it. And as he did so, his hand brushed the firm swell of her breasts. She shuddered, her gaze fixed on the necklace and not on him.

The intimacy was shattered by panic screams. The townspeople, led by the militia, poured into the hall. Soon it was chockfull. Then silence fell. Only the murmurs that occasionally swept through the hall suggested the presence of people. Otherwise a profound silence reigned, heightened by a miasma of sweat and the obnoxious smell of fear. On the grass field around the hall and along the ochre road that flanked it, the townspeople had gathered, waiting for William to speak.

Slowly his gaze swept the crowd and settled on Old Kapu, who was curled up on the floor with a bunch of militiamen breathing down his frail neck. The old man, confronted with that predicament, seemed as mesmerised as a squirrel before a famished cobra. The Lebanese wore the expression of a man who, unable to persuade his captors of his innocence, was dumbstruck, bewildered. Boley, Tetese's father-in-law, was still in his working clothes. With him was his entire household.

'Where is the carpenter?' William asked.

Silence followed his question.

'Where is carpenter Seleh?'

Suddenly a batch of militiamen, led by Corporal Gamla, tore away from the crowd and rushed up to him. One of them lost his step and fell, his rifle clattering on the concrete floor. When Corporal Gamla stood before William and saluted him, he broke into gibberish.

'Speak up clearly, Corporal!'

'Chief, he's locked himself up in his house.'

'I want him here in ten minutes.'

Shortly afterward, a tremor swept through the crowd as the carpenter was ushered in, handcuffed and naked except for a pair of boxer shorts. William envied him his good looks: a chiselled, well-wrought body like an elaborate handiwork of the gods, a height that emphasised his defiance, and a face full of transient but calculated emotions, a rebel to be admired or despised. William despised him now. But what intrigued him most was the carpenter's gaze: it was fixed on Makemeh.

'It's all because of her, isn't it, Chief?'

'What do you mean?'

The carpenter chuckled, like a man conscious of an advantage over an ignorant opponent, and with his eyes still locked with Makemeh's he said in a slow and matter-of-fact voice: 'Just ask her and she will tell you, Chief.'

'You are the one in handcuffs, Seleh. I decide what happens here.'

'Oh, yes?'

'Yes.'

'I hardly ever make a mistake – ask her.'

It was at this point that Makemeh's composed face broke into smithereens of rage, but it was William who translated her expression into action. When she turned to him, her gaze as hard as granite, he jumped off the podium and faced the carpenter. Slowly, almost theatrically, he cupped the carpenter's chin in his left hand and lifted it so that he was gazing right into his nostrils, where he could see a scattering of salt and pepper hair, and some dry snot. From that angle, the face looked ugly and deformed, and it was gurned with helpless fury. It spat and grimaced but was unable to free itself of the hand that held it.

Then William dealt it a neat blow that sent the carpenter crashing on the concrete floor. Quickly he was upon him. Tears of rage streamed down his feverish cheeks. Overwrought, his nose dripping, his whole composure shattered by that violent outburst, William went on battering the carpenter. The town hall was quiet. No one stirred.

'Tell me, Seleh,' he panted as he chased him in the space between the crowd and the podium. Every time he caught up with him he threw himself on him. 'Tell me what happened.'

In the end carpenter Seleh slowly rose to his feet, as if a rib or two had been broken in his body, and he drew himself to his fullest height, ever defiant. He was ready. The town hall held its breath.

The carpenter spoke in a slow, calculated and almost detached voice, a derisive smile accompanying his every word, as though he'd not suffered a beating. He recalled the time Tetese returned after months of absence. It was a troubling period to which everyone in and outside that large hall could attest. But what made it so remarkable and unforgettable was Makemeh's visit to him.

'She came to see me one afternoon, Chief.'

Makemeh did not twitch a muscle.

'She came disguised as a man.'

CHAPTER 12

'Tetese had returned with an army,' carpenter Seleh told William in front of the crowd, 'an extraordinary event that would be surpassed that same day by another: the reaction of the townspeople.' Most of them, torn between the desire to take to the mountains and the longing for answers to questions that were as relevant as their safety, had braved it to the main road. How did a mere storyteller manage to raise such a force? And what were the soldiers doing in Wologizi? Standing under a drizzling sky, the crowd had searched the past for answers but had only stumbled upon a footnote about a man some of them had once wronged but not in such a way as to justify an invasion. So, as the long convoy of dark jeeps and dull-green army trucks snaked its way through Wologizi, one of them asked aloud the most important question on everyone's mind: *Who was Tetese?* No one could answer that question because Tetese had already become a myth.

Meanwhile, one of the townspeople had already had an encounter with the soldiers. 'It was me, Chief,' Seleh said. The carpenter told William that he had driven that very morning to the mountains to fetch some timber, as was his wont. On his way home, one of the soldiers, a bulky man in a spotted black-green uniform, his gaze as dead as a seasoned torturer, had hauled him out of the car and had stood him upright. The soldier had mounted an automatic on the carpenter's shoulder and had fired into the silent air until the magazine was empty. Cheered on by his comrades, he had reloaded the machine gun, had switched to the other shoulder and had pulled the trigger, howling with enthusiasm. The gunshots had turned the carpenter deaf in one ear.

Carpenter Seleh told William that whenever this period was recalled, Corporal Gamla would often claim that he was the first to see him wobbling down the muddy hill like a drunkard. The policeman's first reaction had been to burst out laughing because a drunken carpenter Seleh was a rarity, but something in his bearing had checked him. Rushing to his help, the corporal had suddenly stopped midway, had turned about and had taken to his heels. It was not cowardice that had forced him to make a run for it, he would later insist to anyone willing to listen to him, 'but the terrifying sight of soldiers pouring down like vultures upon Wologizi.'

On that day a deep darkness had descended upon Wologizi, caused not by an eclipse or a deluge of rain but by advancing jeeps and trucks crammed with soldiers. Hundreds of townspeople who had gathered along the road to receive Tetese, had followed the corporal eastward, far away from the advancing troops, for at such precarious moments any semblance of authority, even that of a mere corporal, is revered. But from that direction too sirens had blared.

The soldiers had by then cordoned off Wologizi. They'd taken positions at its every exit: at the town centre, the mansion and the town hall, at the front and rear of every home, along the main road, and around the cinema and the Lebanese's shop. The men had moved about in dark sunglasses, flourishing glinting weaponry, their proud steps demeaning anyone who crossed their paths. They'd whispered to their walkie-talkies as though imparting terrible secrets to invincible figures at the other end of the line. Then, suddenly, with a swiftness as effective and as efficient as the fear they had sowed in the hearts of the townspeople, the men had rounded up every individual in Wologizi and had gathered them up in and around the town hall. Only Tetese's wife was allowed to stay at home, guarded by a soldier.

Then Tetese had revealed himself. The crowd had seen him alight from a dark, armoured jeep, and he had mounted a flight of steps with assured steps into the town hall and onto the platform.

Tetese was never known as stylish. Never before had he exuded such confidence. Moreover, the once thin and emaciated Tetese had looked as plump as a village toad in less than a year of absence, his cheeks a hefty round of flesh. He had smoked a pipe, a replica of the Old Man's. In his right hand Tetese had held a staff – a collection of feathers, bristles and amulets – which many would later credit with supernatural powers. Most conspicuous of all was his outfit: the short gown and trousers, dipped in the yellowish dye of kolanut, were bullet-proof – no knife, cutlass, dagger, spear, or witchcraft of whatever type could harm him. Tetese had returned an invincible man.

The crowd had watched him descend the podium, one step at a time, and edge his way through them, his nose sniffing the air like a predator in search of a prey. On reaching Old Kapu, he had stopped. Tetese had seemed aware of the old man but had not gazed at him, or addressed him, and then he had made a sudden about-turn. Soon he was on the podium again, settled leisurely in an armchair. Then he had folded out the dreaded staff neatly on his lap.

'Bring him to me,' Tetese had ordered.

The soldiers had bound Old Kapu's hands behind his back, his ribcage visible under a thin layer of skin, taut as a drum exposed for hours to noonday sun. 'I would like to see what becomes of that chest when hit by a dagger,' one of the soldiers had joked.

'We meet again, Old Kapu,' Tetese had said.

This was followed by a long silence, during which Tetese had spat a mouthful of phlegm at the old man but had missed. Ordered to erase the gob, Old Kapu had stepped on it.

'I have a favour to ask of you,' Tetese had said, pausing once again, a new method of speech he had certainly rehearsed and mastered wherever he'd been. 'I've been away for a while to think things through, to ponder on my life amidst you people. Tell me why you are here, old man, and I swear on the lost grave of my beloved mother that I'll let you go.'

Old Kapu had been about to speak when Tetese had jumped off the podium and had alighted before the crowd. 'That goes for all of you here. I'll let the town be if one of you can tell me in all honesty why you've all been summoned to this hall.'

The crowd had remained silent.

'You refuse to tell me.'

The crowd suffered his gaze, which was particularly piercing and intense, pulverising their strength to encounter it. Even while he felt the gaze, Old Kapu had found it hard to believe that the look of a man he had known all his life could take on such hardness. This had led him to the conclusion that refusing Tetese a roof could not have been the sole reason he'd been singled out. So the old man had swallowed hard and had whispered: 'It has to do with your mother.'

'What on earth do you mean?'

Old Kapu had then revealed what Tetese already knew. That once he had been married to Tetese's mother, a marriage that abruptly ended when a stranger had snatched the woman away from him. As suddenly as the stranger had appeared he had disappeared again. No one knew anything about him, except that he was a man whose orders were obeyed, a talent he had employed to seduce Old Kapu's wife. 'He had then left her with a child who would later be called Tetese,' carpenter Seleh said.

William gestured to the carpenter to stop.

'I've heard enough of this, Seleh,' he said.

On turning to Makemeh, William could see nothing in her face to indicate that she had been touched by the story. But Old Kapu was clearly affected: he sat on the floor of the town hall, not stirring, as if life itself had left him.

'So all along you've been withholding this important fact from me, Old Kapu,' William said. 'This makes you the prime suspect. You had a motive to hate the child who could have become yours. You will tell me what happened to Tetese.'

Old Kapu looked stricken, as though struggling with words he was unable to properly articulate. His head raced with confused thoughts; the hall swam before him.

'What have you got to say, old man?' William asked.

Old Kapu was silent.

William told the militia to take the old man to the mansion where he would have a face-to-face talk with him.

Then he turned to the carpenter.

'What did Tetese do thereafter?' he asked.

'On leaving the town hall that day,' carpenter Seleh continued, 'Tetese, who was carried in a hammock, went to his one-room mud house where his wife awaited him.

In the presence of the townspeople who bore him and whose impromptu praise songs accompanied him – songs in which he was celebrated as the Chief of Chiefs, Warrior of Warriors, The Invincible, The Merciful, The right and just ruler of the forest region, The chief adored by all and without a single opponent – Tetese entered his modest hut. The soldiers stood at the door, guarding it. After more than an hour Tetese emerged with tears in his eyes and the news that his beloved wife had died in his arms.'

'Indeed, killed, Chief,' the carpenter said, his eyes fixed on Makemeh, as if he were solely addressing her, his lips parted with a lecherous smile, the gap in his teeth as bold as ever.

'There is a difference between dead and killed.'

'Yes, there is, Chief,' the carpenter said. 'Tetese told us that on seeing him, his wife had choked to death in a paroxysm of joy. The town was forced to mourn her death for a whole month. The grief-stricken threw themselves on rain-soaked roads, smearing mud on their faces. They cried till their eyes were swollen and their voices clogged.

'Then Tetese went on a vengeful spree. He carved those lines on his father-in-law's face and wounded and maimed hundreds. He was simply unstoppable. One time, he forced worshippers to bow in the dust for twenty-four hours only because he wanted to see how quickly God answered a prayer.'

Hard on the heels of her mother's death, the carpenter told William, Makemeh had come to see him. It was around dusk, and he was leaning his arms on the railings of his veranda, looking at life unfolding before him in Wologizi, life under Tetese's tyrannic reign. In the far distance, he had seen the figure of a man in a suit, and only when the figure approached him did he realise it was Makemeh. Perhaps, he had thought, the disguise was meant to evade her father's soldiers who were keeping curfew.

'Makemeh entered my house, Chief, and I followed her. What I saw took my breath away: your precious Makemeh was standing in my bedroom stark naked.'

CHAPTER 13

Makemeh sprang from the podium and flung herself at carpenter Seleh. She scratched his face with her fingernails and sank her teeth with feral brutality in his chest. All the while, even as he bled, his blood spattering on the dusty concrete floor, the carpenter wore a triumphant smile on his face, as though all along he had been herding the crowd towards that particular climax.

William ordered the militia to take him away and lock him up in the police cell.

As he was being led out of the hall, carpenter Seleh yelled out something which made the crowd shudder: 'I should have done what I had decided to do with you the day you came to see me, Makemeh. I should have killed you.'

It was too much for Makemeh. In a fit of hysteria, she tore at her plaited hair, thrashed about on the floor, beating it with her hands. She gave full vent to her rage with an unbearably piercing shriek and then suddenly fell down in a faint.

'Somebody should help her,' a woman cried.

In response to this, a bevy of women shoved a stupefied militia aside and crowded about Makemeh. They denied William access to her when he descended the podium to attend to her. She had become their sole concern now, the women told him, and whatever bond he might have forged with her was shivered until she stepped out of their midst.

The heat had eased up, so had the sunlight. And except for the main entrance to the hall and the square-shaped perforations in the walls which still allowed in some sunlight, dusk had cast shadows on almost everything. William climbed up on to the podium and waited for Makemeh to come to. When she did, he instructed the women to take her to the mansion, and he dismissed the crowd.

The Lebanese joined him on the podium and squeezed his arm amicably, his face flushed. 'What about dinner at my place?'

Despite the fact that he mistrusted him, William agreed because the Lebanese was an outsider like himself. Moreover, the man feared him more than anyone else in Wologizi. When the Lebanese left and the hall was empty except for the militia, the corporal approached William as though he was about to whisper a secret to him: 'Everyone agrees that the carpenter should be locked up, he's hated so much.'

'I know you don't hate him, Gamla.'

'That's because he's the only man in Wologizi who's not afraid of speaking his mind, Chief. One can accuse the carpenter of anything but the truth that he speaks. It hurts like a boil, Chief.'

'What he said in the hall could not have been the truth.'

'Makemeh is… '

Corporal Gamla caught William's gaze and kept silent.

'Tell me, Corporal, speak up.'

'She's a very complex young woman.'

'In what ways?'

'Just consider her reaction in the hall. Why react like that if the carpenter was not telling the truth?'

'She was being disgraced before the whole town!'

'Yes, but such a reaction, Chief!'

Corporal Gamla stopped short of telling William that this Makemeh was a dangerous woman, one he himself feared because a daughter of Tetese was capable of anything.

On his part, William wondered how the corporal behaved when not with him. Was he then in league with the carpenter? Could he and his militia turn against him? How loyal was he actually?

The militiamen were singing a song about an illiterate soldier who murdered his way to power. Though he loathed them with all his heart, William knew that he needed them if ever he was to achieve his goal in Wologizi.

'Call them up here,' he told the corporal.

The militia filed in two columns behind Corporal Gamla and marched towards the podium to another song about a man who set fire to his own house and waited in the darkness, hacking away with his cutlass at those who came to put out the fire, all because the town had wronged him by being silent when a man eloped with his wife.

'We are going hunting tonight,' William told them.

He caught in their eyes a hunger for action, and so he promised them the one thing they desired most: 'Once again, I give you my word that if you do what I say, which means doing what the Old Man says, then I'll make each one of you a commander of your own militia.'

The men followed him out of the hall and into a dusk lit dimly with bulbs that were suspended from trees and thin poles along the road. Before them, against a horizon splashed with fiery colours, the mountains were still visible, and below them Wologizi was in an anticipatory mood.

They were all ascending the hill up to the mansion when William caught a faint but unmistakable sound, which reminded him of those that had terrified him the other night. He stood still and listened, and indeed it was true. The sound came with the wind – a drawn-out, plaintive and utterly despairing cry which rose just above the noise of Wologizi. It was answered with a deep chorus of voices that swelled in an incessant chant. Once again, those strange, unfathomable sounds threw him into panic.

'Did you hear that?' he asked his men.

They listened, but except for the wind which at that moment was rustling through the grasses, they heard nothing, and told him so. In fact, the wind soon ceased. Convinced however that his hearing had not betrayed him, William decided to track down the source of the sounds. He raced down the hill with his men, their rifles cocked to the ready.

Even when they were in Wologizi proper, the noise did not cease; on the contrary, they intensified, challenging him, testing his resolve. He hurried on, almost breaking into a run, his heart pounding hard in his chest. Soon, he located their source – it was Old Kapu's place. The noise gathered pitch as he led his men to the front of the house. Then they ceased with an abruptness that hit him like a slap in the face. For a while he was confused as to what to do, and then he climbed the steps and crossed the long corridor. The compound was empty except for one person.

Seated on a low carved stool, shelling peanuts was Hawah Lombeh. She turned to him, as though she had been wrenched out of a trance, surprised but pleased to see him.

'Where is everybody?' William asked.

'I should be the one asking you that question because you were the one who ordered the entire town to gather at the town hall. I must say I was surprised by your action. Was that necessary?'

'Why were you not present?'

She did not answer him. Hawah Lombeh seemed mainly concerned about him, worried because he looked so exhausted.

'Wologizi seems to wear you out,' she said.

'They definitely came from here.'

'What do you mean?'

'The sounds, those damned sounds.'

He left her to search the compound for traces that could indicate that the noise had indeed originated from that place but found nothing. Silence reigned everywhere. He returned to Hawah Lombeh and sat on a stool facing her, his mind befuddled. How could he explain this phenomenon? Was he imagining it? But that could not be because he felt saner than ever, and he was conscious of this. He was not insane.

Insanity, he believed, was the loss of the ability to reason as he was doing now. He knew that the mystery of the auditory phenomenon was connected with Tetese's disappearance.

Hawah fetched him a calabash of water.

'You need to rest for a while,' she said.

The water was cold. After drinking it in a single swallow he regarded Hawah. The skin between her brows was furrowed, the same expression his aunt would wear when worried about him. She sounded like his old aunt now when she said: 'The heat here sometimes drives people out of their minds. I suggest you rest during the day and go on with your work only at the end of the day.'

He thought of what had happened between them.

'Tell me if it was true what you told me last night.'

Hawah Lombeh nodded.

'But it's daylight,' she added quickly. 'What we say at night should never be repeated in the day. Save it for tonight.'

'No, Hawah, it cannot wait.'

'You are in such a hurry. Here in Wologizi events unfold of their own accord, we never hurry them. It's almost night.'

'Were you telling me the truth?'

'The sun has yet to set. Whatever I tell you now would mean nothing, would carry no weight, because I would say it only to please you. The darkness emboldens me, brings out the best in me.'

'Something terrible is happening in Wologizi,' he said, and was surprised by the terror in his own voice. 'It has to do with Tetese's disappearance, I'm sure of that now. You see, I hear sounds. Last night I heard them and today also. They originated from here.'

'They must have been my songs.'

This explanation sounded so absurd to him that all he could do was stand up and move towards the corridor. Hawah Lombeh pursued him and threw herself between him and the door. She held him by the arms to prevent him from leaving, and he could see the panic in her eyes, as if of all things she could not bear it to see him upset.

'What did I say to make you so angry?' she begged.

'The sounds could not have been yours because I heard them from a distance as far as the town hall.'

With that he shoved past her to the door.

'Don't let your anger master you,' she said.

The militia were daydreaming about a career in the army when they saw the man who would make those dreams come true. The men jumped to attention and saluted him, their voices in unison, disturbing the twilight silence. They were heading towardss the mansion.

'Go ahead, I will join you later,' William told them.

It was almost dark as he hurried towards Old Kapu's house and hid behind one of the trees before it.

The waiting was brief. Soon he saw Hawah Lombeh come out of the house, with one end of her waistcloth in her mouth, chewing on it, deep in thoughts. She gazed left and right before branching off in the direction that led out of Wologizi to the capital. William followed her and hid behind a tree, from where he saw her join the old men under the breadfruit tree. The men had been in the town hall but William had not paid much attention to them. On seeing her, the old men created a space for her in their midst, and they began to crack jokes about her. They said that she could hardly wait to abandon her frail husband and elope with the stranger.

Because she did not laugh at the jokes, the men turned to the subject of William. 'So you think he's alone?' one of them asked.

'Such men are never alone,' another said.

'I guess there's an army waiting behind the mountains for a signal from him to reduce our town to rubble,' one said.

'Stop talking such nonsense,' Hawah said.

The old men, to William's amazement, became quiet. Just then Hawah Lombeh stared in the direction of the tree behind which William had hidden himself, and he thought she was aware of his presence.

'Why don't we ask Mr Mawolo himself?' she said.

The old men turned to her, surprised. William was about to escape when she called out to him, and he was forced to emerge from hiding.

'So, tell us, Mr Mawolo. Do you have an army stationed behind the mountains with the intention of wiping us out?'

'What are you doing among these men?'

'They are the town elders, and once every while I mingle with them so that they can tell me what I need to do to become a better wife to my old husband. But now they all believe you've swept me off my feet, and I'm ready to elope with you. What do you think?'

'What I think is that you are all hiding a secret from me. I promise I shall never leave Wologizi until I unveil the nature of that secret, and if I do you will know what manner of man I am.'

'What do we have to hide?' Hawah asked.

'The circumstances around Tetese's disappearance. I have your chief in custody, and I'll compel the truth out of him.'

'So you are holding my husband prisoner?'

She was still referring to Old Kapu as her husband, this woman who had lain with him not long ago. He was furious with himself for having discerned in her a trace of his aunt.

As he left her to join his men at the mansion, he could not but derive some consolation from the fact that the townspeople thought he had an army at his disposal stationed beyond the mountains. With that belief, he thought, he could never fail in Wologizi.

Despite the darkness, he could still see the road and the dimly lit mansion in the distance. At a certain point he heard footsteps behind him but did not look back because he thought it could be nobody else's but Hawah Lombeh's.

CHAPTER 14

Most members of Kapu's household had gathered within the walls of the mansion. On seeing William, they hastily bowed in supplication, begging him to let the chief go, and some even followed him upstairs to the living room where Old Kapu was confined. The old man looked serene, beyond pain, and only his mouse eyes, slightly dilated, betrayed some emotion. He had been tied up in such a way that both his knees, pushed up towards his chest, almost touched his chin.

'Have you thought things over, old man?'

'Yes, why listen to a man who chose an effeminate as a houseboy?' Old Kapu asked William, referring to the carpenter. 'What Seleh does with that boy… terrible if you were to ask me.'

The living room was silent.

'Leave us alone,' William roared.

Hawah Lombeh, who had indeed followed him to the mansion and had since been fussing about her husband, refused to leave.

'Then stay and watch by all means,' he said.

She knelt beside her husband, whispering kind words to him. She tore at the rope, but was unable to untie it.

'You are a coward, Mr Mawolo,' she said.

'Behave yourself, woman!' Old Kapu snapped.

'Tell your husband to be honest with me, Hawah. That would save your tears. Ask him to tell me the truth.'

'What truth?' the old man asked. 'It is for example true that carpenter Seleh has a rare gift that even the spirits of the forests envy. They taught him carpentry, you know. One day a young Seleh lost his way in the forests and returned months later a fully-fledged carpenter. But instead of making full use of his gift, he goes about tarnishing reputations and making enemies.'

'I want to know about your first wife and the man who left her with the child Tetese. I want to know who he was.'

'A stranger, unknown to all in this region.'

'I'm sure you know more about him.'

'I might just as well tell you more about him, if that is of any help to you. The man was a road-builder, one of those men who broke down the mountains that surround Wologizi and connected us with the outside world. The road-builders were reclusive men; they worked on the road and slept in makeshift houses. They were proud men and often looked down upon us. They regarded us then and now as country people, as backward.'

'How did he end up stealing your wife?'

'Women are capricious creatures, Mr Mawolo. It wouldn't surprise me if when you decide to leave, one or two of them end up following you. They wouldn't hesitate a bit, because you are a man of consequence with a militia under your command. My first wife must have been fascinated with the secrecy about the road-builder, with his pride. Or she might simply have been fed up with life in a remote border town. She was from a coastal town and belonged to a people who worship the sea, who perceive its ebbs and flows and its violent storms as manifestations of love. They have no history of drowning, because the sea, their true love, would always guide them to the shores. My father, who like me and like his father was a town chief, took me on a journey where I met her and married her. I should not be seated in this room, tied up and interrogated like a criminal. I'm the victim here, Mr Mawolo, the one who was betrayed,' the old man said.

Because the heat was unbearable, William went to the windows and bent each glass slab downward, but there was no wind. He was sweating so profusely that he took off his shirt.

'Now, tell me about the sounds last night.'

'I heard that you think it's the work of the Poro,' the old man said and shook his head, denying this. William was not surprised to hear him say that, was not surprised at all that his exchange with anyone quickly spread through the town. Old Kapu was about to go on when the light went out, and after a while it came on again. But as the purring of the generator faded away in the distance, the light dimmed out and would not come on for the rest of the night.

'You are angering the Old Kapu,' William said.

'I heard nothing last night, I swear, Mr Mawolo.'

'You are lying to me,' William said.

Old Kapu encountered this remark with a rueful silence which he later broke with a moan that William mistook for surrender. Several minutes later, however, he still refused to speak.

'You leave me with no other option,' William said.

He asked the militia to light some candles. As one of them fetched him a knife, William thought that things did not happen to people without a cause; in their history and behaviour must lie clues as to their present fate. The clue to Tetese's disappearance and to the auditory phenomenon lay in the obstinate silence of the old man.

So he confronted him.

Hawah Lombeh fell on her knees.

'Please be merciful,' she pleaded.

She threw her hands about him, holding him tightly. The contact briefly reminded him of the night before, and he saw himself wavering. But at a sign from him, the militia grabbed Hawah Lombeh and led her out of the room, leaving him alone with Old Kapu.

'Open your mouth, old man,' he ordered.

But Old Kapu clenched his teeth. William pried them open and brought the tip of the knife to rest in his mouth. Old Kapu, now paralysed with fear, his mouth bleeding blood that glinted in the candlelight, felt his strength abandoning him. 'Speak up, old man,' William said.

To allow Old Kapu respite, he relaxed the tension of the knife against his mouth. Only then did he realise that the old man had passed out. When he finally did come to, the old man was unable to speak or even move. William asked the men to take him away.

'You, Gamla, come here,' he roared.

When Corporal Gamla saluted William, he seemed as subdued as a soldier about to be reprimanded.

'Stop playing the fool and tell me what I need to know.'

'What about, Chief?'

'About Tetese, you blockhead.'

'All I can tell you is that after months of absence, Tetese returned as a paramount chief and with an army. He was sent by the president to implement order, but there was order, Chief. I was in control. Tetese brought vengeance and chaos with him. Power consumed him.'

'This sounds ridiculous,' William shouted. 'The president would never send anyone but a competent person. The

Old Man could not be involved in such a petty drama. It's beneath him.'

Refusing to listen to any more of the lies, William longed for some consolation and knew exactly where to find it. He left the men and went upstairs to see Makemeh. A candle in hand, he approached the bedroom. The peace he encountered on opening the door and seeing Makemeh calmed him. With this woman, he thought as he approached her, he would want to spend the rest of his life.

She was stretched out on the bed, sound asleep. Her head was cuddled by one arm, her lips slightly parted, and her skirt exposed part of her legs.

Try as he might William could not reconcile the sleeping form with the violence he had witnessed in the town hall. It was a contradiction that made him hesitate, but the peace that reigned upon her and her extraordinary beauty exorcised his doubts. So he approached the bed.

She did not stir until he sat beside her, and when she spoke her voice was drowsy with sleep.

'I was never at the carpenter's.'

Clearly the words pained her; her face wore a frown which transfigured his own into a similar expression, both refuting the carpenter's claim that she had ever been at his home. In her eyes, which burned steadily under his gaze, he caught the glint of outrage at such an assumption. He nudged closer to her, feeling her warmth. Beauty, he thought, manifested itself most powerfully at close range. Makemeh's face seemed preserved despite that harsh environment of hard sun and rain.

Trickles of melted candle glided onto his fingers, but he gulped down the pain in order not to disturb the gratifying moment. Overwhelmed by it all, William vowed to punish the carpenter one way or the other for besmirching her reputation.

'I'm going to see him tonight,' he said.

'You have to put a halt to his fabrications.'

She was about to say more but he placed his finger on her lips, which felt soft and brittle, trembling slightly under his touch.

Sated by this brief interaction, William hurried down to lead his men out of the mansion, en route dinner with the Lebanese and then a confrontation with the carpenter.

CHAPTER 15

The hill upon which the mansion stood sloped down to a valley of swamps from where the road took off in a slight hillock towards the town centre. These swamps, rich but largely uncultivated, formed a boundary between Wologizi proper and the hill with the mansion, radio station and town hall. A mass of thatched huts was perched on both sides of the road, connected by a stream. That night the swamps throbbed with the chattering of insects and the cries of famished children. It was here that the darkness spewed out a remarkable figure: the carpenter's houseboy.

William's torchlight framed a face with bold eyes that nevertheless expressed an endearing softness, the mouth mirthful, on the verge of laughter.

The young man seemed to have been waiting for them, and his impatience was clearly visible because he could not stand still. On seeing him, Corporal Gamla rushed to him, about to slap him.

'Don't you dare, Corporal,' William said.

The policeman was taken aback, and this perhaps emboldened the young man to say: 'I don't know why he's so pent-up, sir.'

'Chief, let me teach him some manners,' hissed the corporal.

'The Chief is not stupid, Gamla,' scoffed the boy.

The boy whispered something to William, who told the corporal and his men to wait for them, and he followed the youth.

The path the two took was bordered with clusters of tiny vegetable gardens and led to a thatched hut. Inside, three stones formed a fireplace, and on a wooden pole hung a hurricane lamp, a clutter of utensils and all manner of leathery pouches. Showing William to a mat, the young man took a seat on another, facing him.

Scents of damp mud and wood that made up the wall, some of which had been nibbled by termites, teased William's nostrils, and he began to sneeze.

They were not alone. On a mud bed attached to the wall a girl lay asleep under a single piece of cloth. She awoke with a moan and sat up. She was a lanky creature who exuded a musky smell of sex. The smell forced William to regard her: she was young, he could see that, perhaps of the houseboy's age, and frail, her pert breasts barely concealed, her drowsy eyes gazing with contempt at William.

'Don't mind her, sir, she lives off me.'

To this remark, the girl sucked her teeth. She seemed indifferent to the purpose of William's presence in that hut and went on to tie her head-gear slowly, fasten her waistcloth about her and saunter out, but not without flashing William a hard gaze. He could not understand the source of her contempt for him, and was still thinking about her when he heard the militia accosting her.

'Make sure the girl is left alone, Gamla.'

The hurricane lamp cast a flickering light on the youth's face. Because he was sweating, his dark skin glowed, and he looked agitated.

There are moments when a gaze transcends the ordinary to become a medium through which an entire story is told.

The young man's gaze revealed its true nature to William, and this made him uncomfortable.

'I know how much you hunger for the truth, sir. But there's no way you can unravel the mystery around Tetese's disappearance. You would have to wipe out the entire border town, the entire forest region, and even then no one would tell you about Tetese's fate.'

William sat upright, struck by the force of the young man's words, their implications overwhelming him.

'Why is that?' he asked.

The youth did not answer immediately. Fear threw his mind into a labyrinth of conflicting emotions. One aspect of it incited him on and the other cautioned him, so that he seemed unable to muster the courage to go on. He fetched a gourd of palm wine, took large swigs, and wiped his mouth with the back of his delicate hand, and then in a trembling voice said: 'Because something binds them that is stronger than death, sir.'

'Tell me what it is,' William said.

The young man lifted his eyes to meet his own, and for a while their gaze was locked. Just as he was about to speak, his jaws dropped and a painful cry escaped him. William turned to see the girl standing at the door.

She'd been listening in on them.

No amount of persuasion could make the young man part with the secret that night, and William left the hut empty-handed.

Over and over, he thought about the force the youth had described, a force much more powerful than death that controlled the entire forest region. And once again, he thought of the Poro.

CHAPTER 16

The Lebanese was about to close up for the night when William and his men walked into the shop. The man was hauling in bags of rice and other products, like cement and large utensils, which had been on display outside the shop. William wondered why he had not hired a helping hand. At that hour of the night, the shop was flooded in a yellowish light, as were the homes surrounding it, a stark contrast to the rest of Wologizi. 'The lights in those houses are powered by my generator,' the Lebanese answered to William's inquiry. 'I make sure there is light every night, and I charge them for it, Chief.'

The militiamen were appraising the goods.

'Keep your hands off them,' the Lebanese snapped. Except for the Chief, he told them, none of them were invited to his dinner. The men did not object. 'All that garlic and onions only make the mouth stink, you know that, Baldhead,' one of them said.

They mocked the shape of his nose, which was crooked like a beak, and they referred to his failure to satisfy his skinny wife who in the end had abandoned him. 'He doesn't know that skinny women are insatiable,' one of them said, and the rest broke into laughter.

'Get out of my shop,' he roared.

The living room, to which he led William, was decorated with various pictures of snow-capped mountains and ancient ruins of Lebanon. Framed portraits of family members stood in dark corners as though he'd chosen to forget them. From a cassette recorder, Arabic music blared. Above the main door hung a silver-gold ornamented dagger – 'a family heirloom,' the Lebanese told William, 'which is more than four centuries old.'

These things, remarkable as they were, did not compete in grandeur with the picture that faced William on entering the room. It was of the president. The tobacco addict was dressed in a made-to-measure suit, and was waving his pipe at a hysterical crowd, his lips pursed, as if he had just drawn on the pipe, a glint of mockery in his eyes.

The Lebanese showed William to a seat at the dining table and fetched him some ginger ale. He nodded to the music, crying out the lyrics, as if a memory long forgotten had been evoked by the singer. Through the opened windows, a gust of fresh wind drifted in from the valley. 'Here we are, two strangers in Wologizi,' William thought. It led him to think about the other stranger, the road-builder, whose action was still having its repercussions in that forest region.

The Lebanese shuttled between the kitchen, where he was preparing dinner, and the living room.

'I was told that Tetese's father was a road-builder,' William called towards the kitchen, and he heard the plates clattering on the floor. 'Do you know that story?' he went on, knowing that he had caught the Lebanese off balance.

The man entered the living room. 'Yes,' he said and inclined his head towards William. 'Some people in this town even believe that the road-builder and the president are one and the same person.'

William grabbed the Lebanese.

'Do you know what you are saying?'

'Yes, that's what the townspeople are saying, because they are unable to explain Tetese, a man who was once nothing but who suddenly became so powerful. It all has to do with the ignorance of these forest people. For lack of an explanation, they invented one. Because you see, Chief, Tetese has to be explained, he has to be understood, his true nature exposed to us all. Otherwise we are left with nothing. Otherwise we feel cheated, made fools of.'

When William let go of him, the Lebanese downed the glass of ginger ale in one swallow and disappeared in the kitchen. 'This border town has been in rebellion for ages,' the man called out. 'What if the Old Man, to mock his enemies, had chosen a failure to head them? No insult is more painful than investing a man who means little in a society and who's seen as idle, stupid and ignorant, with powers beyond anyone's dream.'

William was silent, for what the Lebanese had just said did not correspond with the reality in Wologizi, a place full of the president's portraits, unless the portraits were meant to conceal their hatred of the Old Man. But what about the mansion, that imposing edifice built in his honour? If it was true that the townspeople were as recalcitrant as the Lebanese claimed, then the Old Man, who had dispatched him, would have certainly told him, or at least given him a hint.

Meanwhile the Lebanese, who watched his every move, interpreted his silence to mean that he had finally convinced him, that from now on the stranger would rely on him and turn to him for advice. Sudden joy welled up in him at this thought.

Because in the town hall that day, when he had seen how William had reacted to Makemeh, going as far as fighting on her behalf, he had decided to protect him from her. 'Makemeh has a history, too, Chief,' he said and paused for effect. 'She's having an affair with the carpenter. She's in league with him. Tetese's daughter conniving with a man who would gladly trade his craft for an opportunity to hurt anyone in Wologizi – just imagine, Chief.'

'But that's not why I'm here,' William said. 'And even if it was true, things are not always the way we see them.'

The Lebanese had returned from the kitchen and was standing at the other end of the dining table with a pot of spicy sauce in hand. He was struck with a premonition that William was about to alter the course of his life forever.

'I'm here because I thought you've changed your mind regarding the role of the auditory phenomenon in this town. I thought you had invited me to tell me all about it, Baldhead.'

Slowly the Lebanese set the pot on the table, took a seat and unfolded his hands, palms upward, the four stumps as grotesque as ever.

'You see these, Chief?' he said, gazing at William. 'Well, each stump represents a story Tetese told us that night. If I were to touch upon what you've just mentioned, my fate would be worse than the loss of four fingers.' The Lebanese went on to add that on leaving his own country more than three decades before, he had searched for a place to set up business. Wologizi had fitted that profile. Being a foreigner, he had constantly swung, like a pendulum, between the fear of incurring the wrath of his host country and the knowledge it would never happen.

'So, please don't force me, Chief,' he pleaded.

'I won't leave this room until I'm told.'

The Lebanese sweated, in spite of the cool wind from the valley, and his hands were unsteady: they would steal nervously under the table, would reappear and hold a glass, toying nervously with it.

Exasperated, William approached him.

The Lebanese recoiled and collapsed on the floor, his legs flying about like a severed lizard tail. 'You look just like him, Chief,' he cried. 'You look just like Tetese when he chopped off my fingers in this very room.'

William thought, as he watched the Lebanese writhing on the floor, that it was a theatrical display intended to distract him.

'Now, are you ready to talk, Baldhead?'

Taking sides in any dispute, the Lebanese realised at that point, was just another way of exposing one's weakness to the mercy of the other to be exploited at will. Was William blind? Couldn't he see that he was demanding the impossible of him, of everyone in that forest town? In the end, realising he had no choice, the bald Lebanese wiped the sweat off his face, and said slowly: 'The noises you heard the other night were intended to force you out of Wologizi.'

'But, I'm here to stay,' William bellowed.

There was defiance in his voice, and he seemed unperturbed, his eyes sparkling. For a while, the Lebanese believed him, and even thought he was invincible. Yet, his association with William had only rewarded him with uncertainties regarding the solid wall of existence he had built in that town. Now all he could think of was how to salvage what was left of that wall.

Meanwhile William was musing on what he had just been told. If the sole purpose of the auditory phenomenon was to hamper his investigation, then he would stay up all night with his men to identify the forces governing it. No force could counter or defeat the deadly effect of the gun: it had built and broken empires. In the end it would protect him more than any other thing. On pausing in his thought process, he was immediately overwhelmed by thoughts of Makemeh. She was the lull in the storm of events with which he was being confronted. She was always on his mind, but the Lebanese's comments disturbed him. Perhaps, he thought, the clue to the entire mystery lay in Makemeh's relationship with the carpenter.

He could not wait to find out. So he left without dining and sat down on a bench outside the shop, under the beam of an unsheathed bulb, waiting for his men. He thought of the first time he had seen the carpenter with Makemeh, imagined what had been exchanged between them. He thought about the spectacle in the town hall that day and how it had forced him to resort to violence – all these events led him to conclude that Makemeh was the key to the mystery and the carpenter the door. He was jolted out of his reverie by a cat which alighted before him from the shop's attic, nibbled its right paw, glared with its marble eyes in his direction, and then with a bound became one with the darkness, out of range of the light. And still Makemeh was feverishly on his mind. He had to do something to get rid of his doubts.

He listened to the tense silence of Wologizi until he heard his men and saw them enter the sphere of the light.

The men had gone to see Tetese's father-in-law, had searched his house and had found a huge pantry full of rice and other foods. They had looted it. The father-in-law, they told William, had accumulated his vast wealth through a severe regime of saving. He had begun with fetching and selling firewood and had gone on to build dozens of homes which he rented out with an exorbitant increase in percentage every year. Once he became wealthy, he turned into a thief, an exploiter, a blood sucker, a man who had learned to handle money with a monkish sobriety that had earned him the nickname: 'the Miser.'

As he listened to them, William envied them their simplicity. They were like dogs that needed only to be fed, even with leftovers, to be forever grateful. 'It's time we visited the carpenter,' he said.

CHAPTER 17

Carpenter Seleh was very cooperative and spoke readily, unlike earlier that day. Since the incident at the town hall, carpenter Seleh had been confined in the police cell, and now as he spoke William could not but wonder about the authencity of the information imparted to him. Obviously when it came to Makemeh, all the carpenter did was provoke him, William realised this as he listened to him. But what Seleh did not know was that Makemeh had ceased to be his soft spot. In fact he had distanced himself from her, uprooting every iota of feeling for her from the depth of his being, so that what remained was only his curiosity as to her role in the drama that her father had become.

'Only after your Makemeh left my house that night did the urge to kill her take hold of me, Chief,' carpenter Seleh told him. 'I had darted out of the house with a cutlass in my hand, intent on carrying out what I had not done while she had been with me. Soon, I saw her hurrying along the main road, bathed in the silvery hue of the moon, her steps quicker, deprived of any grace. For the first time, I realised that Makemeh led a double life: that of a graceful young woman in the presence of men, but in private awkward and simple. Fully aware of the danger of being caught by Tetese's soldiers then keeping a twelve-hour curfew, I raced towards her. And do you know what I thought as I ran,

Chief? I thought that perhaps she was in league with her father, for she was one of the few who had not incurred his wrath. Finally, I caught up with her, and she turned and faced me.

The carpenter paused and asked William for water, but as there was none he took up the thread of his narrative.

'In her eyes and across her lips lingered a haughty smirk, Chief,' the carpenter said. 'You never know what will follow such nasty expressions as hers until you see it – and then you are hurt and you suffer. She drew herself to her full height and thrust her bosom towards me, her breath rapid. She pushed against the cutlass I had brought to rest on her left shoulder, pushed it so hard that, at the encounter of blade with skin, she moaned. The blade dug in her flesh, and she bared her ivory white teeth, her eyes glinting with provocation. With her right hand she pressed the cutlass hard against her skin and felt with a finger the blood which glinted in the moonlight. She showed me the blood, Chief, and then, from deep down within her, issued forth a swooning sound like that of a mating lioness. I wavered, and she broke into laughter. At first it was just a soft chukle, and then she laughed loudly. 'I always knew you were a queer, Seleh,' she said and left me kneeling in the dust.

It took a while before I could haul myself up and chase after her, determined to put an end to my torments. Shattering the silence of the night by calling out her name, I pursued her to her grandfather's house. I awoke the household with my hard pounding on the door, because at that moment I had ceased to care. Tetese's soldiers, alerted to the noise, encircled me. One of them hit me so hard that I realised I had lost consciousness only when I woke up in the very cell in which you are standing listening to my account, Chief.'

William did his best to conceal his uneasiness, but the story had touched him to the core. That Makemeh was capable of seducing men, he knew from first-hand experience, but that she could have collaborated with her father was new to him. Until now, he had not found a shred of evidence to support this claim, and if indeed she had supported her father the townspeople would not have allowed her to continue living among them. Carpenter Seleh was a man of fantasies but was right in one aspect: Makemeh was a young woman with many faces. William went back on his first conclusion that she was the key to the mystery and Seleh the door. The reverse was true.

'What happened after that, Seleh? I suppose you were released afterward?' William asked.

'Indeed, the next day I was out. Thanks to Makemeh who put in a good word for me. Her influence is far-reaching, Chief.'

'But why?'

'That was the question I kept asking myself, but I didn't have to wait long for an answer, because that same night Makemeh came to see me, this time in her own clothes. She sauntered in my room and took them off, but by then I felt no desire whatsoever for her. Strange, isn't it? I must own that once upon a time, I was in love with her. She was a great flirt, your Makemeh. She would raise my hopes only to dash them later. I had seen her grow, seen her chest sprout into firm buds. And her cheeks, puffy with pubescent vigour, gradually and inevitably take on permanent outlines that transformed her face into the arresting aspect that you've come to treasure so much, Chief.

She was the only woman who kept me awake at night, not because I wanted to possess her, but because I wanted to know her, know the source of her charms, her power over men. I wanted the impossible, her love. Sometimes I wonder whether someone had ever tasted her love or will ever do, for that young woman is precarious.'

When she stood before me naked that night, there was no craving left in me, only the stark reality of a woman reduced to simplicity by her very nakedness. She fascinated me, she still does, the same fascination that once led me to carve a sculpture in her image – the epitome of my work – which my houseboy had the nerve to steal. It was not lust for her, Chief. I simply, simply hungered for her body the way I hunger for my houseboy's every night.

So when she stood before me, when she offered herself, I knew right then that her action had a price tagged to it.

'Do you know what she asked of me, Chief?'

Once again, there was that mockery in his voice.

'She asked me to kill her father.'

This turn of events shattered every possible explanation and turned everything on its head. William was thinking quickly.

'Why would she ask such a thing?' William asked. 'First you thought she was working with her father, and now this.'

'Because Tetese killed her mother.'

William had to own that the man had a way with him, often astounding him with his revelations. Until that moment, he would never have imagined, despite his doubts about her, that Makemeh would have treaded such a path, or taken such a decision.

'Your Makemeh is capable of murder, Chief.'

'It's said that Tetese disappeared.'

'Like thin smoke in the wind.'

'Then your accounts are contradictory.'

Carpenter Seleh laughed.

'That's because I refused to carry out her request,' he said. 'I felt I was being manipulated by that woman of yours

– just as she's using you now to get to me. So be on your guard.'

Instead of fulfilling her request, the carpenter told William, he had rallied a handful of people to resist Tetese's tyranny. The resistance had supplied the town with food, thus undermining the curfew which had laid siege on it for weeks. Wologizi would not quake under any pressure. But the supplies had depleted and the siege had compelled the townspeople to feed on cats, dogs, insects, rats and wild roots. Hunger had led to the failure of the rebellion.

'Because of this, Chief, I became a traitor in the eyes of the townspeople. I was accused of being responsible for their sufferings. And Tetese, the man who began it all, was forgotten. Such is the nature of the people of Wologizi.'

The urge to confront Makemeh with all his doubts overwhelmed William now. He imagined her and the carpenter together: the carpenter drawing her to him, leading her to bed, stretching his muscular body along her slender one, both throbbing with the fever of anticipation, and then both bodies intertwining, the entire act long and passionate, and then followed ultimately by her request. No matter how hard he tried, he could not get rid of that disturbing image.

William heard himself asking, 'What happened before her request?'

Carpenter Seleh was silent.

'Answer me, Seleh!'

The carpenter withdrew into the darkest corner of the cell, and William regretted asking the question. He turned around and headed for the door of the cell, as though to escape. Then carpenter Boakai shouted: 'The thing you expect of a couple – a good fuck.'

William stormed out of the police station.

CHAPTER 18

The man who had visited Wologizi and unleashed a series of events that culminated in his storming out of the police station was determined to squeeze a confession out of Makemeh. As he led his men to the mansion, he could not but imagine the picture the carpenter had sketched of her, of a depraved woman, and yet she claimed never to have been at his place. These contradictions, all the contradictions of recent days, enraged him so much that he failed to see the mud-bricks piled up along the roadside until he tripped over them and fell headlong, the sudden impact with a brick causing a cut in his lips. He bled like a slaughtered hog, and he thought he could hear Hawah Lombeh laughing, or was it Makemeh? He would have her locked up in the same cell with the carpenter. The militia, wary of his wrath and confused as to the cause of his rage, refrained from commenting and watched him grope among the scattered bricks for his torch. Failing to find it, he snatched Gamla's from him and broke into a run.

Something was clearly amiss. The mansion, which had been left with candlelight burning in some of its rooms, was now swathed in absolute darkness. William and his men rushed in and shone their torches on a face with a pepper-and- salt beard, Tetese's father-in-law. William inquired what he was doing in that house. Boley answered that he had come to report the behaviour of the militia. According to Boley, since William's arrival, the men had turned lawless. They had plundered his pantry and had beaten him.

William ignored him. When the candles were lighted, he saw Makemeh seated on one of the carpenter's chairs, her arms folded about her chest, her lips as firm as the lid of a palm wine gourd. She seemed so collected that she grated on his nerves.

'You come and turn our lives upside down,' the father-in-law went on unperturbed. 'It takes men years to generate the kind of fear you've succeeded in sowing in every one of us in just a few days. Even my granddaughter constantly fears incurring your wrath.'

'Shut up!' William bellowed.

He rushed at the man who, instead of cringing, gazed up at him, his scarred cheeks puffed out in a challenge. Boley looked like a man who had nothing to lose, a man who had become fearless.

'I want to have a word with your granddaughter.'

'You are following the wrong trail, Mr Mawolo.'

The right trail did not lead to Makemeh, the father-in-law told him, but to the bald Lebanese who had usurped the town's economy, stealing the very property on which his shop was built. Boley added that close questioning of the Lebanese would reveal some startling information, for after all it began with his bargain with Tetese. 'From the very beginning that bald Lebanese made some seedy deals with Tetese and his army. He should be the target of your investigation.'

'What did the Lebanese have to gain by Tetese's disappearance, if I'm to believe what you've just told me?'

'Maybe Baldhead wanted to lord it over us?'

'Maybe, maybe – that's the only thing I've been hearing for the past days: everyone trying to lord it over everyone else.'

'I tell you. . .'

'Shut up, and let Makemeh talk.'

'My opinion is no of consequence, Mr Mawolo,' she said.

She sat bolt upright, her forehead furrowed with intense concentration, gazing at him. On seeing William enter the room, trembling with rage, Makemeh had realised that things were not going according to plan, for she had pinned all her hopes on a man whose constant outbursts were clouding his judgement.

'You claim never to have been at the carpenter's.'

'So you went out to disprove me.'

'Were you or were you not at Seleh's?'

At this point Boley stood up and gestured to his granddaughter to leave with him. 'She's suffered enough tongue-wagging,' he said.

'What tongue-wagging?' William asked.

'That you are, among other things, using her.'

'You know it's not true?'

'We judge only what we see, Mr Mawolo.'

Once again he turned to his granddaughter.

'Let's go,' he said.

'Makemeh,' William said, 'I want to talk with you, or else I wouldn't be able to believe you any more.'

Makemeh sat down, telling her grandfather to leave without her. Boley walked out of the room disappointed.

'You have to tell me what you know about your father,' William said, refraining from mentioning the incident with the carpenter in the police cell.

Outside the militia pounced on Boley, threatening to bleed him dry of the wealth accumulated through the hard labour of many in Wologizi. One of the men reminded him of the theft of sands belonging to him. '*You* are the rogue and not the Lebanese.' Sounds of struggles were heard and a strangled cry for help. The men were battering Boley.

'Let him go,' William said.

Makemeh was in tears.

'Tetese was my father, Mr Mawolo.'

To William it sounded like an admission of guilt to something for which she was not guilty. In fact Makemeh wanted to smooth the way for her most important revelation by sharing with him her early years with her father. Suppressing further tears, she recalled childhood memories punctuated with precious moments of joy, especially when her father told her stories. She remembered him taking her to tap palm wine one morning. He had climbed the palm tree, using a taut rope he had tied around the tree. With his back against one end of the rope and the tree at the other end, he had climbed by grasping the rope with both hands and pushing it upward, pausing at every forward thrust until he reached the top. He had collected the tapped wine in a gourd, had tied it to another rope and had sent it down to her. Then he had taken a place under a palm tree beside her and had begun to sip the palm wine. Gradually his tongue had loosened, not into a rash of insults but in enchanting tales. 'I know people in almost every port of the world,' he had boasted to her and had told her their stories. Those tales were actually journeys that transported her beyond the confines of that forest town and into strange and fascinating worlds.

'My father was not as he's been portrayed by the townspeople, Mr Mawolo,' she said. 'People judge others through narrow prisms of their limited worlds. They accuse others of cruelties which are in fact reflections of their own characters. They call my father a tyrant when they are the tyrants. They say he tortured them when they were the ones who tortured him for years. The father I knew was a loving man, Mr Mawolo. He was also sensitive. He dedicated his life to perfecting the art of storytelling. On more than one occasion, I heard him express his love for Wologizi, despite everything it had done to him.'

'Yet he killed your mother.'

'That's not what happened.'

'What do you mean?'

'I was present when my mother died. She was gravely ill long before my father returned. So there was no question of murder.'

'But your father tortured and maimed and killed others.'

'Wologizi deserved what it got, Mr Mawolo.'

For the first time Makemeh revealed the most powerful force that had driven her since her father's disappearance: the hunger for revenge. She remembered her father telling her how, during his trip around the world, he'd longed for Wologizi. The town had been a love song whose lyrics varied with the days: now joyous and strong, then sad and nostalgic, tearing at his heart, calling to him, wanting to see him. When he returned to it, having sworn never to betray it, Wologizi had betrayed him. It had ill-treated him, a pattern of behaviour that went back to his mother, who had been scorned because of her choice of a stranger as her man. The daughter cited numerous and various instances when her father had been humiliated by the very people whose lives he had brightened with his passionate stories.

'It's this hypocrisy that I loathe, Mr Mawolo.'

The tenderness and the compassion with which she talked about her father touched William, and he thought and even believed that it was impossible that she could be a murderer. Carpenter Seleh had lied to him. But at the same time he wondered whether she was not blind to the terrors her father had practised.

'How can you justify his cruelties?'

'Because he was my father, and I had no choice.'

'Yes, you did,' he said. 'You went to see the carpenter.'

'I was never at Seleh's,' she insisted.

'I don't believe you. I don't believe anyone in this town,' he shouted. Makemeh tried to quieten him, for it was important that he remained calm, for only then would he listen to her and perhaps believe her. She had to make sure that he believed her.

'You killed your father.'

For a while she did not stir, and he approached her and loomed over her, terrible and threatening, blocking the candlelight.

'I did not kill my father, Mr Mawolo.'

He stormed out of the room. She heard him instructing the militia to defend the mansion against any intruder. With those men he sounded confident, powerful, and for a brief moment he was her most effective instrument in her fight against the townspeople.

He re-joined her in swift and certain strides, and when she saw him she was convinced that she could make him listen to her. Her heart skipped a bit at the prospect. Men, she'd learned, were always intimidated by a cool, collected woman, and she had chosen to be such a woman ever since she came to understand her feminine powers.

She stood up, aware of his intense gaze, which burned every spot of her body on which it dwelled, and then she made for the door.

'What are you doing?' he asked.

'I'm leaving, Mr Mawolo.'

'There's the question of the carpenter.'

He went to the door, bolted it, and stood before it.

'You have to persuade me that you were never at his place, were never what everyone in Wologizi thinks you are.'

'What am I, Mr Mawolo?'

She yielded to instinct by approaching him and in a calm voice intended to persuade him she said: 'It is my testimony against theirs.'

She hoped that in those words he would discern her essence, her true self, and she moved towards the door but did not budge. For a moment she thought of telling him about the myth that her father was fathered by the road-builder, who was the Old Man, the president himself. But he would never believe her, would laugh at her, or at worst slap her.

Then her thoughts ceased because suddenly he was upon her. He pulled her by her arms and led her to the sofa.

All his longings for her, all her lies and deceptions, all her manipulative skills, and finally her beauty, so terrific even as he faced her, overwhelmed him. He pounced upon her, cupped her smooth, nervous face in his hands, and parted her lips to reveal ivory-white teeth. She breathed like a conquered animal: quick, hard, and resigned. His hands reached for her breasts, and he found them pendulous like a woman's with a child or two at home. 'So, she's been lying to me all along,' he thought, and at that very moment it seemed that her breasts heaved up, erect and proud, provoking him, playing with him, with his feelings, enticing him, challenging him. In her silence, in the tightly closed eyes and limp body, he perceived acquiescence. He undressed her and parted her legs: a bitter-sweet smell invaded his nose, and he lost himself in that odour until he encountered a membrane of resistance. Still dizzied by the odour, the bitter-sweetness as repelling as it was appealing, he thought that the resistance was due to his own clumsiness, and he went on to break the membrane, as though it were a challenge to his manhood. Blood trickled down the grey sofa, which glinted as brightly as her sweaty face. He had deflowered her. Suddenly his member went cold. The world collapsed on him. Under the weight of guilt and self-loathing, William held his face in his hands, remaining so until the dawn of his third day in Wologizi.

Makemeh had disappeared. No one had seen her leave the house. William raced down the hill with his men running after him. He would find her. He would fall before her and apologise to her, tell her that Wologizi had lied to him. Noon met him on his feet, going up and down the dusty streets, all the while fearing an encounter with Makemeh but knowing full well that he had to do it for his own sake, for his own peace of mind. He combed the entire forest town, and when he was tired and could hardly walk, he went and sat down under a cotton tree on the roadside.

Only then did he realise that he would never find Makemeh because she did not want to be found.

CHAPTER 19

Someone patted him on the shoulder, and when he turned he saw it was Hawah Lombeh. She had brought him water. She sat before him in the dust under the cotton tree, and when a dry seasonal wind started and a down of cotton landed in her hair she made no effort to get rid of it. She was gazing steadily at him, as if bewildered by a man she cared for deeply but who continued to astound her with his behaviour. 'Drink,' she said, and William did. In spite of the fact that her presence always suffocated him, he was grateful at that moment that there was someone within reach to console him. 'Now, Mr Mawolo,' she said, her voice deprived of any emotion, 'it's about time you left our town. It wears you out, and by the look of it, it will only bring you more trouble.'

'I cannot leave,' he told her in the same matter-of-fact tone with which she spoke to him. 'There are questions to which I need answers. Until I find those answers my fate is entwined with Wologizi's.'

She nodded and said: 'Then I will let you two be.'

Hawah Lombeh stood up, tied her waistcloth tightly about her and then took the main road. Not once did she look back. He stared after her, her steps awkward, her clothes worn out – an unremarkable woman in every way, and he pondered on her unusual affection for him. What was it in him that she found so attractive, so invaluable that despite everything he had done to her she still remained generous to him?

Had Hawah Lombeh waited longer he would have told her that he could not leave now, not after everything Wologizi had done to him. The forest town had brought out the worst in him. It was to blame for everything, and the more he thought about its nature the more he was convinced it was sinister. William could not remember ever being violent, and although he was an ambitious man he had climbed up the ladder to his present position in the government without hurting a soul. But Wologizi had made him a violent man with its lies and deceits, had made him commit a heinous crime, destroying forever what was most dear to him: his love for Makemeh.

But it was not too late. He stood up, knowing exactly what he had to do. The clouds had concealed the sun in such a way that it suggested the approach of rainfall, and the heat had eased. The border town looked empty when he walked the main road with his men, as if people were watching him from behind closed doors and windows. Because he was fed up with all the spying, the constant tricks, and the hide-and-seek, he sought out the houseboy in daylight, for he intended for the forces behind the auditory phenomenon to see him doing so. He found him filling up a cistern with water from a well in that swampy quarter. He moved with a lithe soft step, and he bore the bucketful of water on his head with refined grace. William watched him bow over the cistern and carefully pour the water. Then he straightened up, lean and slender like a cane.

The houseboy was visibly shaken on seeing him.

'Sir, I cannot be seen talking with you in the day time,' he said, his slender figure trembling. 'You are endangering my life.'

'Calm down, don't be afraid,' William said.

But he could not get him to calm down. In fact the panicked youth ran from William and closed the hut door behind him. From the hut, his pleading voice flowed, pregnant with fear. 'Please, sir, leave.'

But William did not leave. There were banana plants that surrounded the hut, and he sat with his men in their shade. He could have entered the hut and compelled the young man to tell him everything he knew, but some instinct told him to wait until it was night.

The rain had failed to fall. Instead the sun had brightened once again, heading west now but still fierce and relentless.

The men played checkers in the dust, shouting at each other and cursing. In this way evening closed in on them.

The girl who had been with the houseboy the other night came up the greyish-black path. Scarcely clothed in a ragged shirt that fell to her knees, she walked in jerky steps, as if her legs were incapable of bearing her weight and she would fall any moment. His face lit up as she approached, but she sauntered past him into the hut without a word. Once again she had insulted him with her insolence, with the hate he saw in her eyes, and this confounded him. Later, she emerged with the hurricane lamp and followed the path to town. He thought of following her, but was not convinced it was necessary.

Corporal Gamla asked permission to go with his men to find some food, and although he was hungry William was resolved not to eat until the secret was revealed. He gave his permission, and when silence fell on the hut, he entered it and confronted the young man.

'I have to know,' he insisted.

The young man sighed warily.

'You have to guarantee my safety, sir,' he said.

'Your safety is guaranteed.'

'No, you don't understand.'

He was angry with William for downplaying the gravity of the moment; he toyed nervously with his fingers, and he sweated. It took him a long while to muster the courage to speak again.

'You have to take me away from here, sir.'

'Take you away from here?'

'Make me your houseboy.'

'But I don't need a houseboy.'

William stirred uneasily.

'I saw something the night of your arrival in Wologizi. You see, I was outside when someone of my gender was not allowed to be out.'

William could not follow him.

'I'm considered a woman here in Wologizi, sir.'

Only then did the possibility dawn upon William that the houseboy might not have stolen the carpenter's sculpture, and that he had been punished because he had been out when the masculine forces behind the auditory phenomenon were in town. The young man had seen what was forbidden to a woman's eyes.

'That's why Gamla is so intent on punishing you?' William said.

'Gamla is the worst of them all, sir.'

The houseboy told him that the corporal had once been the head of all the militia in the forest region. At that time, he was endowed with such powers that everywhere he went he was borne in a hammock.

'They called him "Gamla the Torturer."'

'But I thought it was Tetese who had that name.'

'Beware of Gamla, he's dangerous.'

William had toyed with the idea early on that Coporal Gamla was playing the subordinate in order not to arouse the suspicion that he was spying on William, but he had not acted on this idea.

'Will you take me out of here?'

'I'll take you out of here.'

Suddenly the young man reached out in the darkness and touched him, and William flinched. Never before had another man touched him, not in that way. The touch, however, was reassuring, the slender hands surprisingly hard but also tender as he held him.

'It's the Poro secret society, sir.'

'The Poro secret society?' William had excluded that possibility after what he'd seen and experienced. 'You are mistaken. The Poro does not behave in such a way; it cannot be the work of the Poro.'

'Not the ceremonial one of today,' the houseboy explained. 'Not the one you and many others in this country and neighbouring countries know and into which boys are initiated. I mean the most ancient form of the Poro, the one with which the fate of kings and those who had wronged society were decided. It's still practised in this region. That's why no one would talk to you. The border region is governed by the code of secrecy. It's bound to it.'

'How do you know all this?'

'Everyone in this region knows.'

'How can I defeat it?'

'That I cannot say, sir. You have to find a way to do that. Meanwhile, you'll take me with you wherever you go.'

'I won't leave you alone,' William said. But, because he found the prospect of being in the company of the young man unattractive, he added: 'I'll sleep here tonight, before your hut.'

The young man sounded pleased.

Even now, as he sat in that hut enveloped in darkness with the young man, he knew he was being closely watched. This was exactly what he intended. If ever there was a place to meet face to face with the forces behind the auditory phenomenon then it would have to be right before the young man's hut. There, on these swampy grounds, on that unlikely border between the old Wologizi and the new, the battle would be joined.

CHAPTER 20

The men were oiling their guns that night when the girl returned and joined the houseboy in the hut without greeting them. At a signal from William, the men formed a cordon around the hut and waited until Wologizi fell asleep. For the first time in his life William had held a gun. 'Give me your gun,' he had asked one of his men, after they had returned from pillaging the town. Corporal Gamla had handed him the rifle with a grin. The gun felt cold in his grasp, hard like the realisation that his only option was to see the case through to its very end. After being instructed in its mechanism, he decided he was ready. He positioned the gun chest-level, aimed it at a giant cotton tree standing proud and defiant on the edge of a mountain beyond the valley and then fired. The shot snatched a branch off the tree, and the gun-butt hit his chest, an impact that rewarded him with the feeling of invincibility. He was ready.

The night wore on slowly. Insects sang and animals called to each other in desolate, mating cries. The darkness enveloped Wologizi in a deep cloak, as if it was gradually strangling it. Occasionally, an owl would hoot, someone would cough, or the darkness would be disturbed by a distant light careering across the firmament. The men would exchange a joke or two. Though he was tired, William would not sleep. He moved about the hut every once in a while, sharing a few words of encouragement with his men, always reminding them of the prize that awaited them in the distant capital. Then he would return and take his place outside the hut, listening to the night.

They waited until the hen cracked the first egg of dawn, and until an ochre sunlight brightened their faces. The forces behind the auditory phenomenon had not revealed themselves.

Suddenly a cry sounded from the hut. The sight of the lanky girl bolting out of the hut froze whatever feeling that was left in William. She threw herself into his arms, sobbing. Her voice rent the dewy morning air, frightening the birds in the trees around them into flight. The militia tried to restrain her, but at a sign from William they let go of her. She shivered, she wriggled in his embrace, she pounded his chest with her hands and arched her back, as though an overwhelming force was tearing her asunder, violating her. William, who tried but failed miserably to quiet and reassure her, was forced to slap her into docility.

'They've killed him,' she finally said.

William fell on his knees. From deep down within him, he groped feverishly for the sorrow he felt was appropriate to the moment. However, what he retrieved was not the wish to shed tears, but a distilled and refined fury that dictated what he should do to survive that place.

'I'll make them pay,' he assured the girl.

But how could they have reached the boy while he, William, had been awake and on guard all night? Had the girl seen the murderers? He tried to get an account of the incident from her. From snatches of her story he gathered that she'd been asleep when she'd felt the touch of a hand, which had awoken her. Staring at her in the dawn of the morning was a snake with distended cheeks and fierce, diamond eyes. The snake had been in search of the houseboy's smell which had led it to the hut, and it had moved across the flat of the girl's belly, a smooth touch that had made her moan, and it had bitten the young man. 'They sent the snake, they sent the snake,' was all she could say.

William entered the hut. In death the young man looked shrunken, the once serene forehead wrinkled, the mouth twisted, and the neck all bone. The eyes were shut, as if to shun a world that had been cruel to the youth. It required great effort from William not to vomit, and he waited long enough until it was not an affront to the dead or to tradition to leave the hut.

Meanwhile, a considerable crowd had gathered before the hut. The men were bearing their grief in practised silence. But the women broke into wailing so charged with sorrow that it attracted more people who in turn joined in the mourning. On seeing William, the women continued their dirge with unprecedented vigour. They touched him with clumsy hands, called him by exaggerated titles, and attributed qualities to him which he had never possessed. They flung themselves on the muddy ground before him, imploring him to alleviate their grief. 'Let him be,' the men commanded them. But the women held even more tightly to him. William was stunned. They are feigning it all, he told himself. All this exaggerated show of grief and sorrow is intended to fool me, to make me believe what I see. They are feigning sorrow for someone who was never one of them, someone shunned and rejected.

He managed with some difficulty to wrench himself free from their grasp, edged his way through the crowd, and then he turned.

'What was his name?' he asked.

'Gaolo Koelor,' was the answer.

The girl was standing on his left, her tense posture seeming to dictate what was required of him, and he felt every eye fixed on him, waiting for the storm in him to break. But it was the sky which broke first-hand with a distant rumbling of thunder. Rain was threatening to fall.

There was no sign of Corporal Gamla, and when William inquired about him he was told that he'd gone home. He dispatched a group of his men to bring him Old Kapu, the Lebanese, the carpenter, the father-in-law Boley, and all the town elders. Someone had to pay for that murder.

The dry season was yielding to the threat of rain. To William it seemed ages since he had left the capital, for that was what chaos did to a man – it shortened his days, compressing time by simply reducing it to a frenzied anticipation of what the next moment held in store. Remote was the capital now, the past a phantom. Only the present mattered. It incited him to take a firm decision: he would arrest the town's elders, including Old Kapu, the father-in-law, the carpenter, the Lebanese and the corporal, because the crime was committed on the town's behalf.

The militia broke into a song about a soldier who single-handedly wiped out a whole battalion of enemy forces. The men seemed pleased with William and were willing to obey him to the end. They walked along the main street, their gazes vacant, and their singing voices dominant. With them was the girl with a hard, vengeful gaze.

They met Corporal Gamla seated under an orange tree in front of his house, surrounded by a gaggle of noisy children. They were breakfasting. On William's order, the militia fell on him. They deprived him of the only means of defence, his pistol. They pushed him against a brick wall, spread his legs apart and tore his uniform off him.

The corporal's family went berserk, and William only managed to silence them by firing randomly in the air. This sent them scattering about for cover. William slowly approached the corporal and brought the muzzle of the rifle to rest on his mouth. 'So, Corporal Gamla, tell me the truth. You are the one who informed on the houseboy.'

Corporal Gamla denied this.

'I was with you all the while, Chief.'

'You are a man of law, Gamla, but instead of keeping the law you chose to inform on an innocent boy.' William pushed the gun harder against the soft flesh of the policeman's mouth.

'Someone lied to you, Chief.'

By then the family were hysterical, screaming and crying. William went into the house where they'd sought refuge, and he took Gamla along with him. The house had two rooms, each containing several beds placed next to each other. The remaining spaces were cramped full of pots, pans, cupboards and portmanteaus. On the wall, at the far end of the corridor, was the Old Man's portrait. Unlike other portraits William had seen in Wologizi, the president was clad here in a colourful, traditional gown that made him look like an ancient king of a lost empire. The president was drawing on his pipe, his gaze resting like a benevolent patriarch on Corporal Gamla. On his part the corporal bowed his head subserviently, as if he was being honoured.

The corporal's family, a mother and eight children, crowded inside, their faces contorted, their eyes dilated. With each step William took, the children clung closer to their mother. When he approached them, he saw, as he stood before them, tall and threatening, that his presence alone was enough to strike them dumb, to paralyse them, to mark them forever.

The call of his men interrupted him. They had returned with but one person: the bald Lebanese.

'Where are the rest of them?' William asked.

'They've all disappeared, Chief.'

William let this information slowly sink in.

'Someone must have seen them,' he said.

'We've questioned many people,' one of the men said, 'but no one can tell us where they are.'

At that moment, William felt a hand on his shoulder, and he turned to stare into the face of the corporal.

'I know where they are,' Gamla said.

Corporal Gamla was visibly excited, as though he had stumbled upon a rare opportunity and could not wait to betray the townspeople.

'They are all in the mountains, Chief.'

CHAPTER 21

The search for the men began on the edge of the valley at the rear of the mansion. William and his group, consisting of the bald Lebanese, the militia and Corporal Gamla, moved westward towards the mountains. A huge crowd gathered along the road, under the rusty roof of the gas station, and in front of the cinema and the Lebanese's shop. They watched the group march solemnly through Wologizi, and on their faces William saw the tense expression of alert animals, ready to take to their heels at the slightest sign of peril.

William still hoped with all his heart to see Makemeh among them, because such an encounter might lead to some form of communication with her. But she was nowhere to be found.

The group skirted the high walls around the mansion and then faced the valley which separated them from the mountains. The bushes were thick here, and William saw that the dark green which was in the distance had appeared dominating was, when seen closer up, a lush mixture of yellow, green and brown bushes. Corporal Gamla stepped into this panoply of colours, and the rest followed. It was a treacherous descent. At every step, the men held onto a tree or to a branch to prevent themselves from slipping. Some of the trees were thorny or crawled with insects that stung upon skin contact. The scuffling sounds of their footsteps through dead leaves broke the silence of the forest, and the air was pregnant with sharp odours. On collapsing into a bush which fired off needle sharp points, William went into a fit of sneezing. He saw a slight elevation which he took for a high ground, but on stepping on it, it turned out to be a heap of dead leaves. Suddenly the leaves slipped from under him and he glided downward to the foot of the valley.

The trees at that spot were taller, their overlapping branches blocking out the full glare of sunlight. There had to be a river nearby, because from where he lay he could hear its soft and enticing trickles, and it made him thirsty. Hunger twisted his stomach.

'Chief, Chief, Chief. . . ' the panicky voices of his men reached him. They rushed about in a frenzy; found him leaning against the colossal flank of a tree. Ignoring them, he approached the river that was roofed with cobwebs of branches. It had no sandy bank except dark-brown earth covered with dead leaves and branches. Because the banks were high and the water foreign to him, he refrained from going down into it. Being so close to the river but unable to reach it unsettled him. Further upward he happened upon a fallen tree which bridged the river, worn out by footsteps. So the corporal had chosen the wrong path, he thought. He covered a few paces on the tree, bowed and took a handful of water. Only then did he notice the sharp cuts in his palms – perhaps a result of the fall, he thought – but despite the pain he drank his fill.

They resumed their search, silent, overwhelmed by the imposing heights of the mountains and the razor-sharp bushes they encountered. The precipitous slopes hampered their progress. Their breathing, laboured as the ascent became more difficult, betrayed enormous fatigue. Each man seemed confined in his own world, each trudging on despite the scorching heat. Suddenly a wonderful sight greeted them – a huge expanse of fresh, green grasses. Here William stopped. From that height he could see the border town, the houses spread out haphazardly, the bright and rusty zinc roofs protruding from among trees, and the town itself so quiet it seemed to belie its ability to generate a force as frightening as the one he could not wait to unmask.

'Why did you choose to ignore the path that goes through the river, Corporal?' he asked the policeman.

'The forest is full of many paths, Chief. I chose one of the shortest and the most convenient,' he answered. 'If anyone here knows a better route, come forward and tell us then.'

Since the onset of this search, William had been thinking about the mountains as more than just a hiding place. Perhaps it also had to do with the auditory phenomenon. Nothing he'd learned in the Poro had been of help to him during the past days. So he decided, hoping for a clue, to recall every phase of his initiation in the Poro. He began with his abduction in the dead of the night when he was just fourteen and being led with other initiates to a camp in a bush, where for weeks he was fed daily with succulent dishes. Occasionally, he was taught something basic, like solving riddles; his back and arms were disfigured with crude ritual scars, a process that had been painful and less rewarding. He was taught to believe throughout that period that he was being reborn, and that henceforth a new life awaited him. But in the end, when it was all over, he felt and saw no change, only a gain in weight.

There was a hut on that camp to which no initiate but only a selected few of the elders were allowed access. The hut was thought to hold the secret of secrets: the source. Some initiates thought that the hut contained a mask, the most fearsome of all the masks that ever existed. Could it be that somewhere in the mountains there was a similar sacred hut with such a secret?

'Why did the elders choose the mountains, Corporal?' William asked, when they'd paused once again, and the men had grouped under a tree, the only tree around that area large enough to offer some shade.

The bald Lebanese who'd been refused a place with them, sat further away on a bed of grass in the full glare of the sun.

'Because there are no better hiding places than in the mountains, Chief,' the policeman answered. 'You have all those caves in which to hide, and you can see the enemy from far.'

Even though the answer was true, Corporal Gamla felt that William was not satisfied, and so he quickly added: 'I know where they are, Chief, and they know that I know. We have to surprise them, and I know how. Just follow me and I'll lead you there.'

'You are one of them, Corporal, so why should I trust you? Why should you help me find them?'

'Because you represent authority, Chief, and my whole life I've been in the service of authority,' he said and turned to his men, who gazed at him with unusual solemnity. 'It's my task to maintain order and to obey my superior.' He sounded as if he had rehearsed the words, and William realised that he was dealing with a man whose actions were dictated by circumstances. However, in this case, he had no choice but to rely on him.

'Was it the same place people fled to when they were threatened by Tetese? Is there a sacred place?'

Corporal was slightly taken aback.

'What do you mean?'

'I know about the source, Gamla.'

Corporal Gamla was astounded. Did William know about the source or was he bluffing? If the former was the case, then the stranger was much more courageous than he had thought. And he decided to tell him something, but not about the source, never about the source.

'The place is here in the mountains, Chief.'

The men were suddenly uneasy, and more than ever William realised how close he had come to the truth. There in the mountains the answer to all his questions awaited him.

'Take me to the source, corporal.'

If the source was an object, like a mask or a totem, or whatever it was that exercised such power over the forest region, William thought, then he would burn it. Then he would capture the town elders, including Old Kapu and carpenter Seleh, and bundle them all off to the capital where they would face trial and be sentenced. But before that, he would ask Makemeh for forgiveness, that woman he'd hurt so much. Perhaps later, when she realised how much danger he'd faced, she would forgive him and would see that he'd not meant to hurt her. So, with a wave of a hand, he ordered his men to move on.

The bald Lebanese lagged behind all the time, and whenever he caught up with them he would shed sharp tears of despair. He became the butt of jokes. At one point, he complained to William, who said he had only himself to blame. 'If you had been honest with me, you could have saved yourself a lot of trouble,' William said.

It took a while for the bald Lebanese to compose himself, but even then his voice broke when he spoke: 'I passed on only what I had heard, Mr Mawolo. I did what I could to survive, Chief.'

The little wind that now and then swept across their faces and which relieved the fatigue had ceased. Every step required great effort. On the crest of one of the mountains, perhaps the highest, the men discovered that they were lost. For hours they'd traced and retraced their steps in a hostile environment only to end up at a spot where they'd been hours before. Corporal Gamla owned to his mistake: it was the wrong place.

William was becoming increasingly distrustful of the policeman, so he brought the muzzle of his rifle to rest against his nape. 'You are lying, Corporal,' he boomed and slapped him. In response to this, the corporal told him that the source was at another place.

'Don't worry, Chief, I'll lead you to it,' he said, nodding to emphasise that he meant every word.

William attached little importance to what the policeman had said, but knowing that the man was entirely at his mercy – he had the gun and the militiamen would not hesitate to go against their commander – he poked him on.

The sun gradually waned. Nocturnal animals began to emerge from their daily slumber, their chattering and plaintive calls overwhelming the silence of the forest. The trees looked gigantic and terrible in their pervasive presence. The men were clearly exhausted, but William chose to concentrate on the task before him: the escapees had to be captured before nightfall. So they trudged on. The dark sky was pregnant with the promise of heavy rain. Corporal Gamla led them to a spot at the peak of a mountain southeast of the border town. He had not misguided them this time.

On the crest of that mountain, he pointed to a light of fire some hundred metres below them.

Obediently the group descended towards the fire until they were just a few metres away from it. From where he stood, William could see a cluster of thatched huts surrounded by mud walls. In a courtyard at the heart of those huts was a circle of men. Among them were Old Kapu, carpenter Seleh and a host of town elders. Seated in the centre of that circle of men was a figure with its back to William. Slowly the figure turned halfway. It was Hawah Lombeh. She was dressed in an elaborate, handmade outfit, her arms up to her shoulders embroidered with pure gold. She was holding a staff. She looked calmed, collected and regal. The gold that hung from her neck and ears and which covered her arms glittered in the last rays of the sun. She was giving orders to the men, and when at a certain point she stood up, a hush descended on the forest. From that distance William could not hear what she was saying, but the gravity of her words and of her presence was felt by them and by those elders who surrounded her.

Nothing had prepared William for this. All the logic of his thinking process, everything he'd assumed about Wologizi, was thrown to the winds. The woman who was insignificant in Woligizi seemed to rule this world, to hold great sway over it, and she looked proud, powerful, and in her element.

'The Source, Chief,' the corporal said.

For the first time, William Soko Mawolo did not doubt the policeman. So, Hawah Lombeh was the Source, the head of an ancient tradition. A woman brought up to be a man.

He could not move, transfixed by the spectacle before him. Hawah Lombeh had by then taken a seat. Two masked figures, one with a mirrored face and the other of a crocodile, had emerged out of the huts. They began to dance before her, honouring her, weaving her name in beautiful songs. Hawah Lombeh raised her head, as if out of intuition, and she gazed in the direction of the group. She had seen them.

The forest began to tremble. The trees swayed as though a storm was gathering force, exposing William and his men to the risk of a tree-fall, which could crush them or bar their way. What he perceived as a storm began to grow in intensity. From all directions came disturbing sounds: loud bellows, plaintive and agonising growls and wailing – all merged into one. One part of him warned him to leave, but the other drew him towards the irresistible ritual, towards the Source, towards Hawah Lombeh.

The nearer he approached her, the more the sounds intensified. He could see her clearly now. She was being borne in a hammock. Was he mistaken, or did he spot the policeman, Corporal Gamla, among the carriers? They were all dancing, their voices rising with a dirge. As he walked on, he could not wait to confront Hawah Lombeh with her love for him, with the womanhood he was sure he'd awoken in her. He, William, would break the Source and relieve her of her power, for he was sure that deep down in her soul she loved him.

It was as if he covered the remaining metres in a cloud of mist, because when it cleared, he found himself within reach of the clusters of huts. The sounds had ceased. There was no sign of Hawah Lombeh, nor of the town elders. The forest was thrown into a strangling silence. No animal made a sound. The men who had followed William breathed heavily, not one of them venturing a word. The Lebanese could no longer withstand the weight of fear; he quaked under it by breaking into tears, whimpering like a child. One of the militia pinched him into silence.

From the right of them another wave swelled. It sounded like the bellows of a thousand horns, or the steady purring of colossal machines digging deep into the earth. The ground shook and the trees cracked. One of them fell before William, a branch bruising his face. Unafraid, ready to confront the unknown, he led his men towards the noise, but just then another wave set off behind them, the most intense of the three. 'Follow me,' he told his men, turning around. He pointed the rifle before him and discharged its content, cutting a path of flame that led them to where he thought the sounds had originated. Suddenly he realised that the men were no longer with him. He called out to them, but there was no response.

All at once, from everywhere, a sustained chorus of sounds swelled, approaching him – all powerful, all overwhelming, and all destructive. They rooted him to the ground, nibbled at his heart which, tinged with fear, pumped loads of blood through his body. The gun fell from his hands. The sounds ate up his strength, overwhelmed him and numbed his legs and arms.

In a final moment of clarity, William understood that he was sharing Tetese's fate. A strange force slithered up to his heart, grabbed it like a pair of hands, and squeezed it with a cruelty that verged on deep tenderness.

He realised suddenly that the cause of his imminent death was not the auditory phenomenon, but his own fear.

From the darkness, a face showed itself, a face he recognised and called out to because he thought it had come to his rescue. His lips formed her name: *Hawah Lombeh*. But it was too late.

When it was all over, silence fell again on the forest. Then, all of a sudden, like a great avalanche, the skies cracked open, releasing an early downpour that heralded the onset of one season and the end of the other.

CHAPTER 22

The sun was at its zenith and did not cast the shadow of the man who ventured out of the small patch of bush where he'd been hiding for the past hour and took the main road. Soon the man was confronted with the remains of what had once been Wologizi. Corporal Gamla could not believe his eyes. In a concentrated operation that had lasted for four days, the border town had been reduced to ashes by an army dispatched by the Old Man to investigate the disappearance of William Soko Mawolo, the man who had been sent to inquire into Tetese's vanishing. Of the once thriving town, there was nothing left but grey foot-paths. The earth was baked by fire, and where homes had once stood were now charred spots.

Corporal Gamla, afraid that the soldiers might return and find him, furtively retraced his steps to his hiding place. The urge to see Wologizi after its sacking had been so overwhelming early that morning that he'd slipped away to be the first to report to the townspeople what had become of their town. On the edge of one of the valleys, at the far end of the town, he took an overgrown and hardly recognisable path towards the river.

The people of Wologizi had regrouped along the banks of the river at the foot of the valleys, an inaccessible spot and the last bastion of defence. The fallen had been given impromptu obsequies, and the wounded were being attended to. Some survivors moved about in a state of limbo, wrestling with the aftermath of the attack. Among them was the Lebanese. He'd been tied to a cotton tree to prevent him from hurting himself. Occasionally, the Arab would break into a feverish chant in a tongue no one could comprehend, or he would linger into protracted silences that were often ignored. Boley, the father-in-law, had been wounded and was lying on a mat. He was being nursed by two women from his once large household.

Carpenter Seleh had been killed during the attack. Old Kapu was stretched out in a hammock, sure that his end was near. 'Carpenter Seleh should have saved himself. That was his problem, his foolish display of strength,' Old Kapu said when Corporal Gamla joined him under the cotton tree and brought up the subject of the carpenter.

The Lebanese began to mutter to himself again, swearing and cursing. He accused the townspeople of conspiring against him, declaring him mad when he was saner than any one of them could ever be.

'Let's not remember Carpenter Seleh as a foolish man, but as a strong man,' Corporal Gamla argued, but Old Kapu disagreed.

Seated under another tree a short distance from them was Hawah Lombeh, closely following the conversation. She had assumed her old role again, of the chief's wife, the obedient, self-sacrificing woman.

Old Kapu, who watched her closely, thought that something weighed heavily on her conscience. They were interrupted by the girl with whom the houseboy had once shared a hut. She passed a calabash of water around. When it was his turn, Gamla asked her to offer it to the Lebanese first-hand. After the Lebanese had had his fill, the calabash was passed over to him. Thanking her with a nod, Corporal Gamla watched her join the other women who were busy with their daily chores. Something greatly troubled the corporal.

'If the houseboy had remained alive, or if he had died by other means, the town would have been spared.'

'It had to be; a betrayal means death,' Old Kapu said.

The old man was staring at the dark green branches of the cotton tree. Hawah Lombeh went and sat beside him. Now and then, his frail hands would lash out at an insect or a fly. Gamla shook his head.

'We should have punished him by other means.'

'No,' the old man snapped, and he sat up and leaned towards the policeman, his eyes burning. 'That was the only way.'

The corporal felt a sour taste in his mouth as he thought about the high price Wologizi had paid, and he was afraid that the worst was yet to come. 'The soldiers will return again,' he said.

'No one can destroy the secrets of the Poro.' Hawah Lombeh spoke for the first time since the soldiers' assault on Woligizi. 'The president knows that whoever leaves the Poro alone will be left alone himself.'

She stood up. There was a stern edge to her voice that silenced the two men. Corporal Gamla knew that it was useless to oppose the president. The Old Man would never leave the Poro alone. He would pursue it as long as he lived and make sure it was destroyed. This was war, and in every war a winner had to emerge in the end. In fact the war had begun a long while ago. A wheel of events had been set into motion by the Old Man with his appointment of Tetese as paramount chief, then by Tetese himself, and then by the proud but short-sighted William. There was nothing anyone could do now to reverse it.

'What do we do with Baldhead?'

At the mention of his nickname, the Lebanese looked up with a vacant stare and then mumbled something incomprehensible.

'We'll send him home,' Hawah Lombeh said.

Corporal Gamla gazed at her, marvelling at the hard expression on her face, not daring to oppose her. The corporal left them and went towards the river, as though he was washing his hands of the harsh course of action that Hawah Lombeh was taking. He had followed her orders and had led William to the mountains. He thought that perhaps what was happening now could not be influenced by mere mortals but by powers beyond them. He knew that he could not escape his lot, which was Wologizi, the town that had made him. He had a past deeply rooted in that forest region, a past that was not particularly colourful but of which he was nevertheless proud.

Old Kapu was troubled by his wife's abstraction. For the first time he doubted her ability to bear the responsibility with which the people had shouldered her. He watched her heading for the river. Since the town's destruction, the river had become the people's only source of existence. Its water was drunk, used to cook and wash laundry. Hawah Lombeh avoided the spots where the women were crowded and went down the river in search of a quiet place to sit and ponder on the changes in Wologizi. Would the townspeople ever lead a normal life again? Would Wologizi ever be rebuilt? What would be the fate of a secret society that had survived the caprice of time? She could not get rid of William's face as death strangled him. The face, which had recognised her in the darkness, had borne the expression of a profound knowledge, as if William had resigned himself to the inevitable. Ultimately he had been consumed by a combination of anger, ambition and perhaps revenge. His obsession for Makemeh had weakened him, and made him vulnerable. Hawah Lombeh had warned him. One of the most important aspects of being a leader, was the ability to wear at all times the mask of calmness that concealed various emotions, including pain. She had to make sure that her pain was never revealed to anyone again.

Hawah Lombeh walked along the river, thinking about the auditory phenomenon, other aspects of the Poro that were inexplicable to even Old Kapu, not to mention the men and women of Wologizi and the forest region; only she knew about them. She would pass on the knowledge to a suitable candidate. More than ever she felt that the time was right.

She headed towards the women who were occupied with different tasks. On her way, she saw a young woman bent over a calabash. Hawah Lombeh recognised the smell of the bitter concoction which was normally administered in small doses to clear the stomach.

The concoction, by the pungent smell of it, had another purpose, and the thought of it frightened her. Frowning with concern, she hastily approached the young woman and laid her hand on her stomach.

'Your child is a gift, Makemeh,' she said, 'not a burden.' She paused and then added: 'I predict a great future for the child.'

Makemeh turned to her with a questioning gaze.

'I'll help you,' Hawah Lombeh said. 'I'll teach you what a mother needs to know. And I'll teach you much more.'

Makemeh let go of the calabash. She thought of the stranger who had loved her but had gone astray in the process, the man who had braved the mountains to meet his fate.

Hawah Lombeh sat beside her and for a long while both women were silent. Then Makemeh laid her head on the lap of that extraordinary woman who began to reveal to her in a soft tone a series of secrets that would change her life forever.

Secrets that were intended only for Makemeh.

Acknowledgements

My gratitude to Yambo Ouologuem whose *Bound to Violence* inspired the title! I met him once in Mopti, Mali, a broken man now but who was once a towering genius of African literature. To J M Coetzee whose *Waiting for the Barbarians* opened my eyes to the possibilities of fiction. And to Alejo Carpentier, the mentor.

Lightning Source UK Ltd.
Milton Keynes UK
UKOW04f0758090415

249354UK00002B/26/P